Alejandro's
Sorceress

A *Warriors of Poseidon* tie-in novella – and -

A *Cardinal Witches* novella – first in the series

ALYSSA DAY

Copyright

Cover design by Syd Gill Designs – www.sydgill.com

Author contact info:
Website: http://alyssaday.com/home.html
Email: authoralyssaday@gmail.com
Facebook: http://www.facebook.com/authoralyssaday
Twitter: http://twitter.com/Alyssa_Day

ISBN: 0985878029
ISBN-13: 978-0-9858780-2-3

DEDICATION

This one is for my readers, who said "Killer leprechauns? Bring it!"

CONTENTS

1

ALEJANDRO cocked his shotgun and followed his teammate into the burnt and jagged opening in the side of the building, hoping that—for once—there weren't any trolls.

He hated trolls.

"Clear," Mac, already moving through the narrow hallway, called back to him. It was Mac's turn to go first. They kept score.

Lately he'd been keeping score on a lot of things. Like time. The year, two weeks, and five days since he'd seen the sunlight outside of the academy, for instance.

Not that he was counting.

Anyway, the course at the FBI's sister division, P-Ops, had kept him plenty busy.

"Shotgun! You coming or scratching your ass back there?"

"No, my friend, I was just thinking of asking your sister to scratch it for me," Alejandro said, grinning at the nickname he'd won for obvious reasons. "She reaches all the itchy parts so well."

"I will kick your ass if you get any of your itchy parts anywhere near my sister. Or she'd kick it for you. Jenny scares even me."

The sound of Mac's Glock firing three shots in rapid succession caused Alejandro to break into a run as he slapped his night-vision goggles in place.

"On my way," he called, not bothering to try to be stealthy. "Save some for me."

He caught the shifting glimmer of light in the corner of one eye and whirled around, aiming and firing in one smooth motion. Whatever it was, he missed. Too short to be a troll, so there was one mercy. If he were the type to have nightmares, he'd still be having them about the last one's breath. Green, moss-covered teeth. What the hell was *that* about? Toothpaste was cheap.

"Shotgun! Could use a little help here!" Mac sounded just the slightest bit out of breath, which was unusual for the man who'd beat the all-time speed record for the FBI's obstacle course at Quantico in an inter-agency competition. Alejandro had won a hundred bucks on that one.

He took off running, cocking the Remington as he moved. The vampire who jumped him five feet down the hall took a blast to the head. Alejandro vaulted over the disintegrating body, not wanting the acidic slime of decomposing vamp on his new shoes.

A high-pitched scream warned him of the approach from overhead of a deadly Mngwa, but he had a silver throwing knife at hand. One lethal toss later, a couple hundred pounds of mutant killer cat lay on the floor, blood gurgling out of its throat.

He skidded to a stop at the end of the corridor, not willing to rush headlong into a blind turn, and Mac called out to him again, his deep voice rough and strained. "Alejandro, if you're coming, now would be a really good time."

Alejandro instantly switched from student-taking-his-final-exam mode to deadly-predator mode. They had a code between them, he and Mac. They were only Alejandro and Maxwell to each other in the event of a dire emergency. Whatever faced Mac around that corner was no training-ground obstacle. Somebody had set a trap, and Mac was caught in it.

Alejandro was going to kick somebody's ass for this one.

He dove for the floor, rolling to the side to protect the Remington, and did a modified army crawl around the corner. The natural expectation was to look for an enemy at man-height, not on the floor or the ceiling. It's why the vampires and other supes who could climb down a building or fly always had the advantage. Nobody would expect a P-Ops rookie to come in at ankle-height.

Alejandro was far, far more than a rookie.

His first glance assessed the situation and told him everything he needed to know. A trio of wolf shifters surrounded Mac, and one of them had gotten in either a good swipe of his claws or a bite—Alejandro hoped it was only claws—and Mac was down and bleeding, his gun a crushed hunk of metal on the floor.

"Come out, come out, little human," snarled the shifter who stood with one claw-tipped foot on Mac's head.

Another was on all fours, his massive head hanging down near Mac's struggling form. As Alejandro watched, that one's long tongue snaked out as he licked blood off the side of Mac's face.

"Yummy," the shifter said in his garbled voice, and then he laughed.

It was the laugh that put Alejandro over the edge. Cool, clear-headed, Paranormal Operations training flew out the window. Hot, primal rage from years of battling murderous vampires in San Bartolo took over. He triangulated his shots in his head a split-second before he took them.

A couple of heartbeats later, three werewolves lay dead on the ground.

"Glad you talked me into that silver shot," he said mildly, as if his partner hadn't almost died and wasn't now in danger of becoming a shifter himself.

Mac forced out a laugh and hauled himself up off the ground. "Damn wolves. I was so focused on the possibility of big, bad, and ugly that I missed the pitter-patter of little feet."

"Brownies?"

"Leprechauns. Bastards tripped me up, and the wolves jumped me when I was down."

Alejandro shook his head and then blasted a hole in the side of the building. Welcome sunlight poured in, and he stepped over the bodies of the shifters to reach his friend. "Let's move."

Mac nodded, but shrugged off Alejandro's hand. "Thanks, but screw that. We're going to walk out of here like it was no problem, and then we'll get me to the infirmary after. I don't want any of those punks laughing at us."

"There are worse things than laughter," Alejandro said, eyeing Mac's wounds. Looked like claws. He hoped.

"Yeah. Fucking leprechauns." Mac bared in his teeth in a grim imitation of a smile. "At least one of them won't be tripping anybody else, ever again."

He jerked his head to indicate the far corner, and Alejandro could just make out a small green shoe pointing at the ceiling.

Alejandro headed for the hole in the wall. He needed to get Mac to the infirmary before anything worse showed up.

"Could have been worse. Could have been trolls."

Alejandro ducked his head to exit the building, so the huge wooden club smashed into the wall instead of his skull.

"Fee, fie, foe fucking fum, little Mayan," the attacker growled in a voice deeper than the interior of a volcano and just as hot.

Alejandro hit the floor and swept a foot at the troll's ankles, sending it crashing to the ground with a resounding thud. With anything that big, the trick was to go for the feet, ankles, or knees. Before he could cock the shotgun, Mac pointed his Glock at the troll's head and shot it through one eye.

Alejandro stood up and nodded his thanks.

"I owed you one," Mac said, but he was now noticeably leaning to the right, and the blood dripping out of his wounds wasn't showing any signs of stopping.

Alejandro sighed. "Why is it always trolls?"

2

Garden City, Ohio

ROSE CARDINAL added a pinch of cayenne pepper for interest as she stirred a potion for sparkling conversation and tried not to glare at her mother.

"You didn't have to call P-Ops for a garden pest, Mom," she repeated for the eighth or ninth time." We could have handled it. Now they're going to put us in some kind of file as nuisances. Do we need to be in a governmental file? No. Look what happened when the sheriff wrote us up for indecent exposure for dancing sky clad at the solstice."

"It's the law," her mother reminded her, also for the eighth or ninth time. "Also, I took care of the sheriff, didn't I? His wife didn't speak to him for a month. Anyway, we have to report any occurrences of potentially dangerous supernatural activity. You can't say this isn't dangerous, after that incident yesterday with the paperboy who was trying to deliver the *Witchcraft Daily News*."

Sue Cardinal might dress like a hippie, but there was pure steel underneath the deceptively sweet face, waist-length white hair, long, brightly colored skirt and dozens of bangle bracelets.

"We fixed him! He never even realized anything happened to him." Rose protested, turning the heat off under the pot and placing a lid on it to trap the aroma inside. The *last* thing she needed around her house was more sparkling conversation.

"Marigold Rose Cardinal, what have I taught you? With great power comes great responsibility," her mother said, untying the red-and-white checked apron she insisted on wearing whenever they mixed spells and potions.

Rose threw her hands in the air. "That's Spiderman. We're witches. And *don't* call me Marigold."

"It's your name. Also, I don't care. I phoned them, they're coming, and that's that." Her mother stalked out the kitchen door, chin held high and an air of injured righteousness surrounding her like the dozens of butterflies that usually flocked to her in the garden.

Rose closed her eyes and counted to ten, then to twenty, before giving it up as hopeless and cleaning up the kitchen. The bright, airy room was her favorite in the entire cottage, which was saying a lot since she loved every single room. She'd painted the walls a sunny yellow with bright white accents and trim, and her sparklingly shiny copper pots shone from the open shelving on one wall.

Her house was tiny, but it was had been all hers for nearly a year now, and after twenty-three years of living with her mom and three sisters, it felt like a paradise. True, a path connected her house to her mom's, where her younger sisters still lived, but it was across the acre of their shared kitchen garden. Right now, during a lovely late spring in Ohio, the garden was blooming so wildly that travelling between houses was almost like crossing a jungle.

"You aren't much like a jaguar, though, are you, Bob?" she asked her black and white cat as he padded into the room, probably from her bedroom, where he'd been napping earlier.

He meowed at her and jumped up on to the cushioned window seat so he could survey his kingdom. She always thought he must have had a little bit of cat royalty in his background, from his regal carriage and "you may pet me now, peasant" attitude, but he, like the house, was all hers. He'd shown up one night on her porch in a rainstorm, tiny and bedraggled, and he'd been hers ever since. Or she'd been his. You could never tell, with cats.

Her youngest sister burst into the house, slamming the door against the wall.

Again.

"Astrid, I asked you not to do that," Rose said, without any real hope that her bubbly sister would pay any attention this time, either.

"They got Ninja," Astrid said, wiping tears off her face with the sleeve of her white peasant blouse. Astrid was the only one of them who'd inherited their mother's sense of style and, at fifteen and long, lanky, and gorgeous, she wore it well.

"We'll help Ninja, honey," Rose said soothingly. "We fixed the paperboy. It's all good."

She wiped her hands on a towel, retrieved a slender glass vial from its position in the refrigerator next to eleven more just like it, and followed her sister outside to rescue the dog.

She stopped on her porch and took a deep breath, unable to resist the wonderful scents of flowers and herbs coming from the garden. Her mother was a garden witch--derogatorily referred to by some as a kitchen witch--and her powers came from spells and potions made from plants.

Rose and her sisters had inherited the same magic, but each of them had something a little extra, as well. In Rose, it was the ability to discover a person's deepest desire within five minutes of being in his or her presence.

Not everyone appreciated this gift; especially since she'd often blurted out her magically acquired knowledge in public when she was a child. Plus, sometimes the knowledge was a surprise even to the person whose desire it was.

That usually turned out badly.

"Rose! Are you coming?" Astrid's voice rang out from behind the small stand of blooming apple trees. "Watch out for the mean one by the tomatoes."

Rose kept an eye out for any strange movement as she headed for Astrid, but the nasty little beasts had learned to watch out for her after she'd thrown an itching spell at the one chasing Bob.

She rounded the corner of the path and found her sister kneeling on the ground beneath a tree, her arms around a tiny stone statue of a pug.

Astrid turned her tearstained face up to Rose. "You have to help my sweet Ninja."

Rose grinned at the sight of the dog, frozen in mid-bark, his tiny pug ears standing straight up.

"I've got it, Astrid. Now stand back." She uncorked the vial and shook the sparkling pink liquid on the statue's head after her sister moved out of the way, and they both watched as Astrid's black pug puppy transformed from a stone statue back into his roly-poly self, apparently no worse for wear.

"Honey, please keep him out of the garden until we deal with this," Rose said, trying to be stern but unable to resist smiling as her sister covered the pup's silky head with kisses.

Astrid promised and ran back to their mother's house, carrying Ninja. Rose watched her and then sighed and turned around to go back to her kitchen and check on her new conversation potion. Their neighbor's son Connor, a very sweet computer nerd and recent college grad who wanted to use it for job interviews, would be stopping by at four to pick it up.

When she reached the cottage, she automatically glanced into the window at Bob and then stumbled to a stop. Her cat, frozen in mid-stretch, had been turned into a stone statue.

Damn garden pests. Why couldn't they get grub beetles or snails, like the typical gardener? Oh, no. Never anything ordinary for the Cardinal witches.

They had to get a freaking basilisk infestation.

3

ALEJANDRO turned the standard-issue sedan right on Wildflower Lane, mentally running through a checklist of the equipment and ammo in the trunk. He and Mac were loaded for bear--or basilisk, to be precise--and yet he still wondered why the regional office in Columbus had assigned two rookie field officers to handle something so incredibly dangerous. He said as much to Mac.

"They know we can handle it," Mac said confidently. Alejandro's partner stared out the window at the tree-lined street with its immaculate lawns and careful landscaping. "It's like a different planet, isn't it?"

Alejandro made a noncommittal noise. Mac had grown up in Vegas, so he was used to desert scenery. Alejandro had been born and raised in a remote village in Guatemala, isolated by vampires from technology or progress, so every place he went in the U.S. felt like a different planet. The computer lab at the academy had been a wondrous revelation, and he'd spent all of his spare time catching up to his American classmates.

Except in weapons training and vampire tactics classes. There, most of his classmates had been forced to work hard to catch up to *him*.

"That's it. 8121 Wildflower Lane," Mac said. "The one set back from the street."

Alejandro pulled in to the driveway while he automatically scanned the area for danger or signs of disturbances.

"Seems like a basilisk would have done more damage," he said. "Or there'd at least be a lot of running and screaming."

"Maybe it ate everyone and moved on," Mac suggested, grinning. "We can go get some lunch and then take the rest of the day off."

Alejandro rolled his eyes. "We'd still have to spend all afternoon writing up the paperwork."

P-Ops was as bad as its parent agency, the FBI, when it came to paperwork. Alejandro's typing was slow, and working on the many reports that came with the job was his least favorite part of his new career. Probably always would be.

They got out of the car and looked around. Alejandro had only taken a single step toward the front door of the small house when a woman who looked like sunshine walked out, and his entire world shifted on its axis.

She wasn't beautiful or even conventionally pretty, and he wasn't even sure what it was about her that had knocked him on his figurative ass. This woman—she was somehow unique. Her hair was a silky fall of golden blond, but her athletic figure was neither model-thin nor lusciously curved. Her face was captivating, though—something about the combination of her individual features packed a punch right to his gut. Maybe her lips, or the strength in her bone structure. Maybe her eyes.

Her eyes.

They were so blue that he almost couldn't believe they were real, and they were snapping with fire, impatience, or annoyance. He couldn't decipher her emotion from her eyes alone—hell, he was lucky if he ever understood *anything* about women--but something about her made him want to spend hours trying.

It took him another beat to realize that her lips were pressed together in a firm line. When she put her hands on her hips—gently rounded hips that clearly had been made for a man to hold--even he, blinded by the most immediate case of raging lust he'd ever felt, could see that she was angry about something.

He tried to focus on the job. He told himself that she'd probably have a terrible personality. He reminded himself that she was a witch, and then it hit him. She projected a sense of power—a feeling of barely leashed magic—that somehow had transformed her into the most fascinating woman he'd ever seen. Maybe it was a spell? She was a witch, after all, and he had never reacted like this before.

His libido didn't care about the *why*. It just wanted to get her naked, which was damn stupid under the circumstances and therefore made him suspicious.

"So. You must be the P-Ops guys. Let me guess; you're from the government and you're here to help?" Sarcasm and something else, maybe annoyance, coated her words, but her voice was musical and so sexy that he wanted to hear her talk all night long.

Well. Maybe not *all* night.

She was breathing hard, and Alejandro tried not to notice the way her breasts pressed against her shirt. He was a professional agent, damn it, not a horny kid. He fumbled for his badge, but Mac beat him to it.

Mac moved around the car, holding out his hand. "Mac Henson and Alejandro Vasquez, ma'am. You have a basilisk problem?"

Right. The basilisk. Alejandro snapped into action and opened the trunk of the car. He pulled out a shotgun, extra ammo, and a helmet with a darkened visor to protect himself from the basilisk's deadly gaze.

"Where is it? Is anybody injured? Any fatalities?" he asked, heading back toward the house.

The woman's mouth twitched, and he could have sworn he saw a smile curve her lips, but it was gone so fast that maybe he'd imagined it. "I'm Rose Cardinal. Are you sure you're ready for this? That might not be enough protection."

Alejandro's gaze snapped to Mac, who strode back to the trunk to suit up.

"We're ready, ma'am," Alejandro said, his confidence in his skills and training overriding his tongue-tied fumbling. She must have put a spell on him. He'd never reacted to a woman at first glance like this before. Not even to Maria.

"Are you presently casting any spells?" he asked bluntly. Surely that much charisma had to be helped along by magical glamour.

She laughed out loud this time. "No, officer, I'm not bewitching you in any way. Don't you have some kind of magic meter?"

He did, in fact, have a dial on his agency-issued watch that reacted with different colored lights in the presence of magic. He'd forgotten about it, like an idiot. He glanced down at it and saw that the dials remained dark. No magic detected whatsoever.

"It's agent, not officer," he said. "But you can call me Alejandro."

"Call me Rose," she responded, and an intriguing hint of pink appeared on her cheeks.

Before he could say anything else, she turned and went back into the house, motioning to them to follow.

"You may as well come through here. I'll call my mother, since she was the one who was so hot to get you people on the job," she called back over her shoulder.

Hot was an unfortunate word for her to use when he was staring at her lushly rounded ass. He could feel his internal temperature ratchet up to about a thousand degrees, and he blew out a deep breath.

Back to business. No staring at the civilian's ass.

He followed Rose into the house, determinedly looking at the back of her head. He glanced back to see that Mac was headed around the corner, signaling that he'd meet Alejandro on the other side. There was no way the basilisk was indoors and, anyway, the woman who'd filed the report had stated that its location was in the garden.

The house was warm and inviting and gave him clues to its owner's personality. A soft cream color covered the walls, which were bare except for a stunning art piece made of glass and aged wood that hung behind the bright scarlet couch. Books were scattered across a brass trunk that served as a coffee table. Framed photos were arranged in groupings on most available flat surfaces; the majority of them featured a variety of blond women who must be related to Rose, although a few were of various cats and dogs.

He took all of that in during the few seconds it took him to cross the room, and then he followed Rose to her kitchen, noting that she hastily closed a door halfway down the hall. The door opposite to the closed one held a small room lined with walls of books. The other one must be her bedroom.

He shoved the idea of Rose in her bed, all that glorious hair streaming across the pillows, out of his mind and watched as she crossed the room to a window seat, where an oddly arched statue of a cat stood.

"Alejandro, meet Bob," Rose said, and he quickly looked around the room, only to confirm that nobody was there.

"Bob? Who is Bob?"

"Bob is my cat," she said, that quicksilver grin again crossing her face and then vanishing. "The basilisks got him just after I rescued Ninja."

"The basilisk attacked your cat after you rescued a ninja?" he repeated slowly, realizing he'd been right. There was no way a woman this beautiful could have a personality to match her looks.

She was nuts.

Totally insane. Probably made up the entire thing as a way to get attention.

"Ninja is the name of my sister's dog," she began, but Mac shouted something from outside the kitchen, and Alejandro hit the door running.

He dropped the safety gear and ran outside into the garden, lifting his gun to his shoulder, prepared for the worst, and wondering why Rose had been so calm when a monster was in her back yard. But he was too late. Mac, pistol in hand, had been transformed into a life-sized stone garden statue.

A small, lizard-like face with an improbably long snout peeked out from behind a flowering bush and hissed at Alejandro, before disappearing back behind the leaves in a flurry of flapping wings.

"What the hell was that?" Alejandro asked Rose, who'd walked up behind him and was staring at Mac with a kind of resigned fascination.

"That was a basilisk," she said, raising one eyebrow and giving him an "are you stupid" look. "Didn't somebody tell you why you were coming? A whole family of them invaded our garden."

12

"But that creature was tiny--I thought--" he began, and then his mind flashed back to the supervisor who'd assigned them this case. He'd kept coughing until finally Mac had asked him if he needed a cough drop, which had made the man turn red in the face, silently hand over the file, and rush out of the room.

Realization hit, and Alejandro muttered a few choice words under his breath in both Spanish and English. The supervisor hadn't been coughing.

He'd been laughing. At Alejandro and Mac, as they discussed all the weapons they'd need for the task. Basilisks apparently weren't huge, man-eating monsters, as he and Mac had thought. They were the size of a chicken.

"Initiation rites for the new guys," he said, half admiringly, half-disgustedly, as he lowered his shotgun.

He turned to Rose. "You called P-Ops for a lizard-chicken?"

She raised her chin defiantly and then nodded her head toward Mac. "Actually, my mother called you. I'd have been happy to deal with this myself. And since it's your partner who's turned into stone, and I'm the one with the remedy, maybe you should be a little nicer to me."

She was right, which annoyed him even more, so he deliberately swept his gaze up her body from her feet to the top of her head before answering.

"Oh, trust me, Sunshine. I'd like to be *very* nice to you."

4

ROSE stalked back into the house, very deliberately not slamming the door behind her. Arrogant, pompous, sexist excuse for a law enforcement officer. Although, from what she'd seen in her very limited experience, those qualities were the norm, not the exception, in men carrying badges and guns. Look at the stupid sheriff.

She calmed down inside the kitchen, and her innate sense of fairness started to kick in. The officers who'd come to the house and told them about Daddy's car accident couldn't have been nicer or more considerate. One of the men--Officer Engel, she'd always remember his name, though she'd only been twelve at the time--he'd sat and held her mother's hand while she cried.

Okay. Fine. Then only Alejandro and the Garden City sheriff were arrogant asses. Although, speaking of asses, Alejandro's was really something to behold. Not that she'd looked on purpose, but it had been hard to miss when he'd run outside to find his partner.

"Why am I even thinking about this, Bob?" she rhetorically asked her stone cat, who naturally didn't answer.

She didn't need the cat's response to figure it out, though. Agent Tall, Dark, and Dangerously Hot was too sexy for his own good—and far too sexy for her balance to remain steady. He was ridiculously good looking, as if Hollywood had cast him in the role of action hero. Muscled in all the right places, silky black hair that was just a hint too long, and dark eyes that looked at her as if she were an especially juicy piece of fruit he'd like to suck between those sexy lips.

Rose stumbled over her own feet when a surge of heat whipped through her at the thought of him sucking on any juicy parts of hers.

"Oh, goddess, I'm in trouble here. Focus, Rose," she whispered to the empty room, more proof that she was losing it, as if she'd needed evidence.

Focus. *Right*. She crossed to the refrigerator and retrieved another vial. At this rate, if they didn't get rid of the basilisks soon, she'd have to make another batch. Not to mention she didn't know if the potion was strong enough to rescue a grown man. The paperboy had been a close one, not that she'd admitted it to anyone. He'd taken longer to transform back from stone to human than she'd hoped.

Plus, he'd refused to deliver their paper ever again.

Ungrateful little monster.

Alejandro walked in, and the air in the room changed and grew heated; charged as if the electric potential of a summer storm had centered itself over her kitchen counter. The skin on the back of her neck tingled with a delicious feeling of anticipation.

Stupid neck.

"Fix him. Now," he ordered.

She threw her best ice-cold glare at him, but he didn't even flinch. Huh. He must be tougher than most people. That glare had scared off one mugger, seven door-to-door solicitors, and three mall product testers.

Rose realized she was mentally rambling, and she shook her head to clear it of distractions like tall, muscular, terrific-smelling P-Ops agents who heated her up in all the dangerous places.

"Excuse me," she said, as she slipped past him in the narrow space between her sink and the center island. She couldn't help but brush against him, though, and she gasped when the zing of electricity from the touch of his chest against her shoulder went straight to her nipples.

She involuntarily looked up and realized that she hadn't been the only one affected. His dark, liquid brown eyes had darkened, and his oh-so-male broad chest expanded as he took in a deep breath, almost as if he were inhaling her scent.

"You *smell* like sunshine, too," he said, so quietly she almost didn't hear him.

Rose inhaled sharply and took a step back. Back away from the crazy man who talked about how she smelled. Who looked like a fierce warrior and dressed like one of the Men in Black.

The dark, conservative suit seemed like a disguise meant to mask the predator wearing it. He moved with lethal grace, but his face had the hard lines and angles of a soldier. Everything she'd never wanted anywhere near her, in other words. So why were her thighs clenching against a rush of sensation?

Right now, those deliciously dark eyes were staring at her with a heat that had nothing to do with anger, and a sense of awareness deep within her went on high alert.

"I can fix him," she said, dropping her gaze; taking the coward's way out of the moment. "I just need another vial of this restorative potion."

She ducked past him to the refrigerator, not sure whether she was relieved or disappointed when he moved back to let her pass.

"That pink stuff will bring Mac back?" His eyebrows shot up. "The sparkly pink liquid in that tiny vial is enough to counteract a basilisk's stare?"

"Well, no, it will probably take at least two," she said, mentally crossing her fingers. Actually, she wasn't as certain as she pretended. Two vials had barely brought the paperboy back. It had taken too long, too, and she'd breathed a deep sigh of relief when he'd finally reanimated.

Mac was a full-grown man. On second thought, she grabbed a third, then fourth vial. Bob still needed to be restored, after all. Her eyes widened when she realized that Alejandro's closeness had driven all thought out of her mind, even her concern for her cat.

Gritting her teeth, Rose berated herself for letting a man mess with her mind like that. She was the reasonable one of the Cardinal witches, after all.

Rose the Rational. The only one in the family with any common sense.

As she brushed past Alejandro again and inhaled his exotic scent of spice and something else—something purely masculine—she resented it all, though. Just once, she'd like to be the wild child. The one who threw caution out the window and ran straight at whatever she wanted, both arms open wide to grab it.

She almost laughed, imagining what Alejandro's expression would be if she dropped the vials and jumped him. The poor man would probably run for his helmet and witch-proof vest.

Still grinning, she knelt down next to Bob and carefully put three of the vials on the floor next to her and uncapped the fourth.

"You're going to help your cat before Mac?" Alejandro's voice held an ocean of disbelief.

"Bob has been frozen longer," she replied evenly.

Holding her breath, Rose offered up a silent prayer and carefully poured the sparkling liquid on Bob's head and then rocked back on her heels to wait.

"Aren't you going to say something?"

Alejandro had moved closer, so the fabric of his pants leg was almost touching Rose's shoulder. She turned toward him to answer, which brought her face just about level with the fascinating bulge in his pants.

She froze, and one of them, possibly her, gasped, and Alejandro quickly took a step back. Rose whipped her head away so she faced her cat, and so Alejandro wouldn't see the blush flaming its way up her neck to her cheeks.

"Be my guest," she snapped. "Try *abracadabra*. That's always a crowd pleaser."

"Look, I didn't--"

16

But the Bob statue finally began to show some movement. At first a shudder worked its way through the stone, and then it slowly dissolved, until only one perfectly furry and very cranky cat remained. Bob hissed at Alejandro and then leapt down from the window seat and stalked away down the hall, head and tail held high to show his disdain for the entire ordeal.

"That took a little longer than I'd like," Rose said, biting her lip. "Will you please grab one more vial out of the fridge?"

She didn't wait for his response, but ran outside, and by the time she began to uncap the first vial, Alejandro joined her. Mac stood, solid and imposing, exactly where she'd left him. Not that she'd expected anything else, but Rose's stomach clenched at the sight of what must be hundreds of pounds of stone.

"I hope that's enough," she said, suddenly very worried.

Alejandro opened his hands to show her that he'd brought all of her remaining vials.

"I figured that if Mac outweighs the cat by a factor of ten or so, you might need all of it," he said, but then he blew out a deep breath. "It was probably stupid. I have no idea how your magic works."

Rose stared up at him, intrigued. A word had been floating around the edges of her consciousness, and she finally realized what it was.

Fierce.

That was the word. Fierce suited him perfectly. He was beautiful and ferocious, and she wanted to run away and step closer all at the same time.

"It was a good idea," she told him, because part of her wanted to soothe and comfort this man who quite clearly had never needed either. Instead, she took a deep breath of her own.

"Let's give it a try."

One by one, she began uncapping vials, pouring each carefully on stone Mac's head. One by one, the potion failed to do anything but drip, in pink sparkly failure, off of Mac's nose and ears and on to the grass.

Finally, when she'd used every drop of potion, she and Alejandro waited and watched for several long minutes. At some point, she realized she was holding his hand—or he was holding hers—and her breath caught in her throat at the feel of his strong, elegant fingers wrapped around her own. At that moment, two things became very, very clear:

Alejandro was trouble, and Mac was still a statue.

5

ALEJANDRO clicked his phone shut and stared at it in disgust. He'd checked in with the office and told them a flat-out lie. Three, in fact. He was fine, Mac was fine, the mission was going great, and very funny on the basilisk.

He stared at the slightly pink stone statue of his partner and realized that everything was very far from fine. Rose had turned about seven shades of pale, yanked her hand out of his, and run back into the house, muttering something about stirring up a more potent spell. Alejandro was back to wondering whether she was crazy or just incompetent.

No. After all, he'd seen the cat transform from an ugly statue to a scruffy and enraged live animal. The potion worked. It was just something in the proportion that was off. Or at least, that was what he had to tell himself, because any other result was unacceptable.

He patted Mac's stone arm. "We are going to fix this, buddy. You can count on it."

Then, feeling like a complete idiot for talking to a statue, he turned to follow Rose inside. A flicker of movement at the edge of the bush where he'd seen the lizard chicken caught his eye, and he whirled around, raising his gun at the same time.

"Oh no you don't, you ugly little flying rat," he said. "Not this time. I've brought the true death to hundreds of vampires. You can bet I'm not going to let a rodent get the better of me."

He rolled his eyes and muttered a string of oaths in Spanish. First he was talking to a statue, and now he was talking to a lizard. Maybe they had special padded rooms for P-Ops agents who went insane on the job.

The basilisk peeked its head out again, and Alejandro pulled the trigger. But just as he fired, a hair-raising scream startled him enough that he flinched and missed his target altogether. The rodent ran back behind the bushes, squawking like mad, and Alejandro whipped his head around to find who had ruined his aim with that gut-wrenching scream.

A blond teenager who looked a lot like Rose was running across the garden path toward him, her hands held up, palms forward, as if to stop him.

"Don't you dare kill him," she shouted. "What kind of a monster are you? A big man like you picking on a defenseless animal. You ought to be ashamed of yourself."

Her lips moved as if she were chanting, but he couldn't hear the words. A moment later, a bright yellow blob of energy, about the size of Alejandro's closed fist, came hurtling toward him. He jumped to one side, and it should have missed him altogether, but the energy ball changed direction midflight and smacked him in the arm.

It felt like a mild shock, but these were witches. Who knew what they could do with their powers? He looked down at his arm, expecting to see a hole burned through it, but found nothing more than a small scorch mark on his sleeve.

The door to Rose's kitchen banged open behind him.

"Buttercup Astrid Cardinal! How many times have I told you not to attack the guests?"

Alejandro turned his head to see Rose standing, hands on hips, on the small patio outside her back door.

"Buttercup? Is she related to you, Rose? Because I think I'm going to have to arrest her for assaulting a federal officer." He aimed a stern look at Buttercup, who was patently unimpressed.

"It's Astrid," she said defiantly. "And you can't arrest me for protecting the wildlife on my own property."

He raised an eyebrow. "You also attacked a P-Ops agent on your own property. P-Ops is a division of the FBI, and both organizations frown on magical attacks on their agents."

Rose walked up beside him and put a hand on his arm. "She didn't mean it; she's only fifteen, and she gets emotional about animal rights. She's been a vegetarian since she was six. Please don't arrest her."

The worry that was apparent in Rose's eyes sent a twinge of guilt through Alejandro. For some reason, he wanted to protect this woman, not add to her stress.

"I'm not going to arrest her, but she might not be as lucky with someone else in law enforcement. I just wanted to warn her about that." He finally allowed the smile he'd been suppressing to show on his face. "I haven't sunk so low as to start arresting children."

Rose blinked, and a hint of pink touched her cheeks. "I ... thank you. I'll have another talk with her about shooting energy balls at strangers."

He laughed -- he couldn't help it. "You mean it's okay for her to shoot energy balls at friends? Family?"

Rose grinned back at him, and she shook her head. "You'd be surprised."

Buttercup Astrid marched up to them, her hands clenched into fists at her sides. "Are you going to stand around and flirt with the hot guy who tried to incinerate a helpless living creature in our garden?"

Rose spun around to face her sister and pointed an accusing finger first at Buttercup and then at Mac. "No, I'm not -- he's not -- forget it. What I'm trying to do, in case you haven't noticed, is restore the man that your *helpless living creature* turned into garden statuary."

The irate teenager finally noticed the statue of Mac, and her mouth fell open. "Oh, boy, we're in trouble now."

"That's what I'm afraid of," Alejandro muttered. He turned to Rose and asked the question, even though he was afraid to hear the answer.

"Are you going to be able to fix this or not?"

"What have you done now? I can't leave you girls alone for five minutes." The woman rushing down the garden path toward them looked a little like Alejandro's village wise woman. She had the same long white hair, the same flowing skirts, and the same expression of serene wisdom on her face, although it was apparent that her serenity had been shaken a little by the sight of the Mac-shaped statue in the garden.

Rose threw her hands in the air. "Mom, I'm not six years old anymore. I just had to stop Agent Vasquez from arresting Astrid, after she tried to incinerate him with one of her defective energy balls, after he tried to shoot the basilisk, after my potion didn't work on his partner. There, are you satisfied? Simple explanation."

Rose's mother blinked, started to speak, and then blinked again.

"Concise, but not exactly simple," Alejandro said. He extended his hand to Rose's mother. "Agent Alejandro Vasquez, ma'am. The statue is my partner Mac. One of the lizards -- *basilisks* got him, and Rose tells me she can bring him back."

"Sue Cardinal," she replied, looking a little dazed. "I still have no idea what's going on, but I'm used to that after more than twenty years with daughters."

She turned to study Mac. "What have you done so far, Rose?"

Rose bit her lip. "Mom, the potion seems to be losing its potency. It took way too long to bring Bob back--"

"Bob? They got your cat? Is he okay?" This from Astrid, of course, who was far more concerned about the cat than about Alejandro's partner. Mac wasn't a helpless living creature in her eyes, after all.

20

Rose shot a distracted glance at her sister. "Yes, Bob is fine. But the potion took longer to work than it should, and then I used nine vials on agent Henson, and nothing at all happened."

Sue's eyes narrowed, and Alejandro could all but see her brain working.

"How old is that potion? If you made it more than three days ago, it loses its potency. Any more than four days and it loses almost all viability," Sue said.

Rose heaved a sigh of relief. "It has been almost four days. That's the problem, then. I can brew a new batch tonight, and we'll have Mac back to himself tomorrow morning."

Alejandro pinned first one, then the other, of them with his most serious P-Ops agent stare. "Can you guarantee it? Because if not, I have to report this to my field office right now. *Dios*, I should report it anyway, but I don't want this on Mac's record, after the--"

He clenched his jaw against letting any more details spill out. "Just tell me that you can fix this. By tomorrow morning."

Sue airily waved a hand in air. "Of course she can fix it. Isn't she the most powerful Cardinal witch to come along in generations? There is nothing to worry about at all, Alejandro. What a lovely name, by the way. Now, what are your dinner plans?"

She beamed at him as if he were an old family friend, and made a move-along gesture to Rose. "Why don't you go change into something nice for dinner, Marigold? I'm sure the nice agent likes to see a woman in a lovely dress."

Alejandro grinned. Apparently meddling mothers were the same everywhere. Rose shot a glare at him that should have blistered his eyeballs, and he quit smiling, fast.

Rose gritted her teeth. "I told you not to call me that, Mother, and why would we care what his preferences are in women's clothing?"

"I don't know why you'd want to invite him to dinner anyway," Buttercup, or Astrid, or whatever the hell her name was, interjected. She crossed her arms over her chest and glared at Alejandro. "He probably wants to shoot Bambi and eat him for dinner. Animal murderer."

"Who is Bambi and why would I want to shoot him?" Alejandro shook his head, feeling an ache starting to pound inside his skull. "Are all witches so confusing?"

Buttercup sneered at him. "Bigot."

Before Alejandro could respond, Sue put her hands on her hips and pointed back down the path the way she'd come.

"Go back to the house right this instant, young lady. I'll deal with you later."

Rose threw her hands in the air. "I've had enough of this. I have a great deal of potion to cook, so I'd better get started."

An extremely loud chiming sound pealed out from the vicinity of the front of Rose's house just then, and Alejandro looked at Rose. "What is that?"

"Oh, no, I forgot about Connor. He's coming over to pick up his conversation potion," Rose said, closing her eyes for a moment. "What else can I possibly have to deal with today?"

"At least my mother isn't here," Sue said, smiling. "She'd drive us all nuts, with her criticisms and suggestions about the basilisk problem."

"Right. We know nothing about interfering mothers, "Rose muttered, rolling her eyes, and Alejandro had to cough to cover a laugh.

Buttercup, instead of heading back toward her house, had been edging toward Rose's kitchen door as they talked. When Rose turned around and caught her at it, the girl blushed bright pink.

"You don't get to be the only Cardinal witch who talks to hunky guys, Rose," she said defiantly. "Connor's really cute, and I know he likes me."

"Connor is twenty-two and far too old for you," Rose said sternly. "Don't even think about--"

Buttercup ignored her sister and flew through the door into the house. Rose, Sue, and Alejandro followed her, but they all froze for a moment when Buttercup started shrieking. Alejandro drew his gun, but Rose put her hand on his arm again. A bolt of electricity seared through him just from that simple touch, but he didn't let it show in his face. It had to be a spell. No way could he be so affected by a woman he didn't even know.

"That was a happy shriek, not a danger shriek," Rose said wearily. Apparently she didn't realize what simple proximity was doing to his resolve not to pick her up and kiss her.

"You're absolutely beautiful," he blurted out, unable to help himself and shocked again at his lack of control around this gorgeous witch with the crazy family.

Sue shot him a speculative grin, and Rose's lips parted and her eyes widened, but before either one of them could say anything, Buttercup came bouncing back out the door, leading a woman who had to be at least a hundred and seventy years old.

Rose gasped, Sue made an odd growling noise, and the old woman flashed an enormous smile full of the whitest, squarest teeth Alejandro had ever seen.

Buttercup smiled happily and put her arm around the old woman. "Isn't it awesome? Granny's here to save the day."

Rose sighed and glanced up Alejandro. "Whether we want her to or not."

6

ROSE wanted nothing more than to spend some quality alone time with the fascinating man who was playing havoc with her nerves and her equilibrium. But of course that wasn't in the cards, tarot or otherwise. Instead of the chance to get up close and personal with Alejandro, who was all coppery skin, long, lean muscles, and wickedly seductive eyes and mouth, she got to look forward to an evening of her grandmother's observations on everything Rose was doing wrong in her life.

Oh. Yay.

Granny perched on the edge of a kitchen chair and focused her bright-eyed stare in Alejandro's general vicinity. She was so nearsighted she often tripped over furniture in her own house, but she was too vain for the thick trifocal glasses she really needed.

"Glasses, Mom," Sue said gently. "You need to remember your glasses."

"Did you pay the cabdriver yet, Granny?" Rose asked, already looking for her purse.

"I think I left my glasses at home, Sue, so don't fuss," Granny said, shooing her daughter away. "And Rose, put your money away. I don't need you to pay anybody."

"You paid for your own cab? Wow, Granny," Astrid said, grinning. "Way to go!"

Granny winked at her. "Now don't get fresh with me, Buttercup Astrid Cardinal. I was paying for cabs and stirring spells when you weren't even a gleam in your Mom's eye."

"We told you that we're happy to drive over and get you anytime, Mom," Sue said, filling the kettle for tea.

"No need," Granny said, flashing her huge denture-filled smile. "I bought a car."

Sue dropped the tea kettle, Astrid high-fived Granny, and Rose stumbled backwards in shocked disbelief, slamming into all those hard muscles she'd been drooling over earlier.

Alejandro, who'd moved behind her at some point after they'd entered the kitchen, caught her with strong hands on her hips.

"I take it that it is a bad idea for your *abuelita* to drive?" he murmured.

Rose went weak in the knees when his breath feathered across her sensitive ear, and she completely forgot what they'd been talking about.

"Um, what?"

The low, rich sound of his chuckle touched places inside her that had no business being touched, especially by an official agent of the P-Ops division of the federal government. She caught her breath before she could moan, or rub her bottom against him, or do any of the fifty other wanton things that her wicked brain was suggesting.

The doorbell rang again, and Rose escaped to answer it before she could do something stupid like start licking the nice federal agent on the neck.

"I bet he tastes as good as he smells," she muttered darkly, throwing her front door open.

The tall, slender young guy who stood there blinked at her. "Um, excuse me?"

"Nothing, Connor. Come on in. Your potion is ready; I just have to bottle it. It's been a busy day." She led him through the house, wincing at the thought of poor Connor having to face both Astrid and Granny at the same time.

"Ah, is Petunia around?"

She glanced back at him and sighed when she saw that his cheeks had turned pink. Yet another conquest Petunia wouldn't even realize she'd made. The middle Cardinal girl was a scholar, first, last, and always, and spent most of her time immersed in the world of ancient books and scrolls. Petunia's picture was probably in the witches' encyclopedia next to the phrase "absent-minded," but she collected admirers like their mom collected butterflies.

Rose sighed. She'd never envied Pet before, but when Alejandro had stepped into her house, Rose had suddenly felt a little bit insecure.

"Right. And I'm not going to let a man do that to me, no matter how pretty he is," she vowed.

"Um, who's pretty?" Connor sounded totally confused, and Rose didn't blame him.

"Sorry. Just thinking out loud," she said breezily, leading him into her crowded kitchen.

"Everybody, you know Connor," she said, waving a hand.

Alejandro folded his arms across his deliciously muscled chest and gave the poor kid a narrow-eyed look. "Connor who?"

"Um, ah," Connor stammered.

Rose pointed at Alejandro. "You. Behave. You don't get to interrogate my guests, especially when they have nothing to do with basilisks."

Connor made an odd strangled sound. "Basilisks? You—um—do I even want to know?"

Astrid sidled up next to him and slid her arm through his. "Don't worry about it, Hotness. We've got it under control. Well, except for the stone guy in the backyard, but he's only a federal agent, so he doesn't even count."

The poor boy's eyes got so big Rose could see the whites all the way around. "The what? I mean, the who?"

"Heh. The basilisk got him? I guess that means he's *rock hard*," Granny said, belting out a laugh that sounded way too much like a cackle for Rose's liking.

Seriously. Witches and cackling? No. Just no.

Alejandro swept the room with his "I'm a cop and I really want to arrest everybody" gaze, and Rose wondered why it gave her shivers in places that had no business shivering.

"I don't even like alpha males," she whispered, whirling around to face the stove and her pot of Connor's conversation potion.

"Ha," Sue said, crowding into Rose at the stove. "That's what I said when I met your father and next thing I knew, I was pregnant with you."

"Mom," Rose hissed, more than a little freaked out. "I so don't want to hear about your sex life."

"She was a wild one," Granny said, suddenly able to hear perfectly for someone who spent a lot of her time yelling "what?" at everyone around her. "I was glad your dad married her before she got knocked up by some wandering poltergeist."

"Granny!" Astrid shrieked, covering her face with one hand but peeking up at Connor through her fingers and looking intrigued. "Poltergeists can have sex?"

Connor stared wildly around, probably looking for the best way to make a break for it.

Alejandro came down with a sudden coughing fit, and Rose glared at him, realizing perfectly well that he was trying not to laugh his ass off at her crazy family.

"You are never going to be invited over here again if you don't behave," Rose told Granny sternly, trying desperately to take charge of the situation.

"Ha! You need a hot man yourself to take the edge of that crankiness," Granny retorted.

Rose's gaze involuntarily went to Alejandro, and his eyes darkened with a surge of heat that nearly seared her clothes off. She raised her chin and tried to pretend her knees hadn't just gone shaky.

"Okay, that's enough. Everybody out," Sue ordered, in full-on *Mom*— or drill sergeant--mode. "Mom, you and Astrid go sit on the couch. Connor, go with them. We'll bottle up this potion and bring it right out to you. It's on the house this time. Alejandro, go—go outside and check on your partner."

While Rose watched in disbelief, everyone did exactly what her mom had told them to do, even Alejandro, who smiled at Sue and touched his forehead in a kind of salute. But when Sue turned to the stove to dish up the potion, Alejandro caught Rose's arm and pulled her along with him. When they reached the door, he bent his head down to hers, and Rose had to catch her breath at the thought that he meant to kiss her.

"I don't know what or why or how, but you are singing along my nerves, *Querida*, and I would be very happy to volunteer to take off any . . . edges . . . that you need me to," he murmured in her ear.

Rose caught her breath as a shiver traveled up her spine from her hoohah. "I don't . . . I don't . . ."

"But I do, lovely Rose. I have no idea why, but I do," he said, but frustration drew his dark eyebrows into a frown, and he glanced down at his watch again. "No magic. How is this possible?"

His accent, which whispered through her like warm honey, deepened, and she had to almost physically slap her unruly hormones to keep herself from falling into his arms. She took a deep breath to dispel the haze of attraction that was fizzing through her brain, but it didn't do a darn bit of good.

"You're not the only one who doesn't understand," she admitted.

His eyes lit up and he laughed, and if she'd though his voice was sexy before, his laugh was sinful.

"I think I'm in trouble," she said.

"I am right there with you," he replied, staring at her mouth. "If I could only--"

But she didn't get to find out what he was going to say, because Granny shrieked and then moaned; a long, mournful sound that snaked chills through the room.

"Not again," Rose groaned.

"Oh, crap, she's having another premonition," Sue said, grabbing Connor's vial of potion and rushing out.

Alejandro followed Rose down the hall after Sue. "What is going on?"

"My grandmother. She's a Seer. And she evidently picked now to gift us with her latest harbinger of doom," Rose said, sighing.

"You have quite a family," Alejandro said, and she almost could have sworn he was laughing again, but she refused to turn around and look at him. Not for the first time in her life, and probably not for the last, Rose briefly wished she'd been born into any other family than hers.

When they got to the living room, Granny was in full bore Seer Mode, which involved her eyes rolling back in her head, her hair floating straight up in the air, and, for some reason they'd never been able to understand, her socks wrapped around her elbows. She was still shrieking and moaning, and Bob was standing on top of the back of the couch hissing at her. Connor, looking terrified, was edging backward behind the cat and the couch.

"Whoa," Alejandro said, stopping suddenly. "This is--"

"Crazy?" Rose supplied bitterly. "Nuts? Bizarre? Ab-freaking-normal?"

"Unexpected," he said, putting his hands on her shoulders. "Is she in pain?"

"No. In fact, she acts kind of refreshed afterward," Rose said, unhappily resigned to the fact that Alejandro would now *never* want to kiss the granddaughter of the crazy seer-witch from the nut job family.

"Mom!" Sue rushed forward and reached out for Granny, and then seemed to realize she was still holding on to Connor's potion. She tossed the vial at Connor.

And then all hell broke loose.

Events unfolded simultaneously, almost in slow motion, and Rose couldn't do anything but watch in horror as Connor tripped and fell into Granny, knocking them both backward onto the couch. At the same time, Astrid leapt through the air, arms outstretched to catch the vial, and accidentally elbowing Sue, so they both fell down, all tangled arms and legs.

The vial, flying through the air end over end, hit the wall and bounced, and the lid popped off.

Rose moaned, clutching her head, as the potion arced through the air in a shining stream and landed right in Connor's face.

Unfortunately, he was holding Bob at the time.

Granny's shriek-moaning cut off mid-screech, and she turned blind eyes toward Alejandro, pointed one long finger at him, and drew herself up. "Your eldest child will rule in an isle of myth," she intoned in a deep, scary tone that was nothing like her normal voice.

Then three things happened:

Granny fell back on the couch and started snoring—loudly.

Connor began to recite the ABCs—loudly.

And Bob started meowing. Also loudly.

"I don't actually have any children," Alejandro said, as if nothing out of the ordinary was going on. "Why is the cat making that noise?"

"It's a sparkling conversation potion," Rose said sadly, wondering where she could buy earplugs. "Takes weeks to wear off."

"To have kids, you have to have sex first," Astrid informed Alejandro. "Have you ever had sex? Do you want to have sex with my sister? She's probably no good at it, since her last boyfriend was a long time ago, and he smelled funny."

Rose sat down, right there on the floor, put her head in her hands, and started to laugh.

"I actually smell pretty good," Alejandro said, and then he started to laugh, too. "You realize that none of this is going in my report, right?"

"I like him," Sue said, grinning.

Rose wondered if there were any spells that could make her entire family disappear. "Abraca-freaking-dabra," she muttered. "Welcome to my life."

7

AN HOUR LATER, when everyone was finally gone and the house was finally quiet, Rose finished cleaning up spilled potion and then carefully discarded her rubber gloves. The last thing they needed was any more conversation, sparkling or otherwise. She could still hear Bob loudly expressing his displeasure somewhere out in the garden.

She sighed and poured herself a fresh cup of coffee, sat down at the kitchen table, and tried to mentally prepare herself to brew more potion when all she wanted to do was sleep.

She looked up, unable to suppress a twinge of hope, as Alejandro came back in from checking on Mac.

"No change," he reported, shaking his head.

"I didn't really expect there to be any. I'll get started on the new batch in a minute. I just needed a caffeine break." She sipped her coffee. "There's more in the pot if you want any."

He poured himself a cup and then joined her at the table and they sat in silence, drinking coffee, and to Rose's surprise it wasn't the least bit uncomfortable. It was almost . . . pleasant.

Something she could get used to. Waking up to Alejandro's beautiful face; drinking coffee with him in her kitchen.

She caught herself before the fantasy carried her away. The last thing the gorgeous Agent Vasquez wanted or needed in his life was a moderately successful garden witch with a crazy family.

The last thing he needed . . . Rose suddenly put her coffee mug down with a thud. "What *do* you want?"

He blinked, and even his eyelashes were beautiful. It was *so* not fair.

"What do you mean? I want Mac to be back to human--"

She shook her head, determined not to let him distract her with important stuff. "No. I mean, what do *you* want? What is your deepest desire?"

A slow, sexy smile quirked up the edges of his lips, and Rose had to clutch the edge of the table to keep herself from leaping over it at him.

"That's kind of personal, don't you think?"

She rolled her eyes. "No. Well, yes, but you don't understand. That's my gift, and I don't feel you."

"You want to *feel* me? This is kind of sudden, Rose, but I have to admit I'm not opposed to the idea," he said, grinning wickedly.

She blushed, but it only made his eyes light up with glee. This was bad. Really bad. Hot guys with great senses of humor had always been her weakness. And this hot guy—oh, boy. He pushed all her buttons.

Distraction again. *Darn it.*

"No, stop distracting me with your . . . argh. No. Listen. My gift is that I can sense a person's deepest desire within a few minutes of meeting him. Or her. Or, um, you. Except, not," she said. Eloquently.

Except, not.

Alejandro stared at her for a few seconds, and then he pushed away from the table and walked over to the coffee pot. He looked really, *really* good walking away.

He poured himself another cup, raised the pot and one eyebrow to ask silently if she wanted more, which she just as silently declined, and then he leaned back against her counter before answering.

"Ah, English is not my first language, so perhaps I don't understand the nuances of what you're trying to say to me," he said, in perfectly fluent English.

Rose blew out a sigh and then laughed. "Hey, I don't think *anybody* would understand what I was saying. Okay, let me try again. My gift doesn't work on you. Your partner, I could read almost before he got out of the car. Connor, the guy who was here earlier? Took under a minute, the first time I met him. But you? I've been around you for hours, and I still don't have a clue."

Alejandro looked intrigued. "What does Mac want? No. Don't answer that. It's none of my business. Which, to the point, is also true of you. Don't you feel like a spy? Listening in on other people's thoughts and desires without giving them back any truth about yourself? It seems unfair to me, Rose."

She looked down at the table, chagrined. Of course it was unfair. She often *had* felt like a spy, eavesdropping on the privacy of others. But she'd been so intent on Alejandro that she'd broken her own number one rule: never to let anyone know about her gift.

"I never wanted this," she blurted out, shame and humiliation burning a path through her stomach up to her throat. "I didn't ask for it. I have tried all my life to be able to block it—to give people the privacy they deserve—but there's no way to stop it. I just *know*. The way you know my eyes are blue. It just pops out at me."

"Your eyes are very, very blue," he murmured, and she glanced up at him and was immediately caught in his gaze. His intense, heated gaze.

"But I don't get anything from you," she said, desperate to clarify. "So, your secrets are safe. Either you're witch-proof, or you don't have a deepest desire."

Alejandro put his mug down on the counter and then turned back to face her, his face suddenly drawn in bleak lines. "I wanted something once. *Someone*. She waited all of three months after I left for the P-Ops Academy before she married one of my friends. So I learned not to want anything too deeply, ever again."

Rose caught her breath at the reflection of remembered pain that vibrated through the air—she could almost taste it, rusty and jagged in the back of her throat. Even a far less powerful witch would be able to tell that here was a man who *did* feel—and feel deeply. She swallowed the lump in her throat.

"I'm sorry. I didn't mean—I'm sorry," she repeated, knowing that she had to keep her distance.

A totally hot guy who was all surface and no depth was easy to resist. Alejandro . . . he was something else altogether, and she didn't want to get tangled up in the net of emotional entanglement. She'd seen what that had done to her mother, after they'd lost Rose's dad.

"It was for the better," he said, shrugging. "For the best, as you say. Maria was afraid of the supernatural, with good reason. Vampires fed on our village for a long time. It wasn't until the Atlanteans came that we finally defeated them. My job would have terrified her, but I was done with simply surviving. I needed to *fight*."

"And so you became a P-Ops agent." Rose understood more than he was saying. For a long time after her father died, she'd thought she wanted to become a doctor so she could save people.

So she could save other little girls' dads.

"So I did," Alejandro said. "Now, shall we make that potion?"

Rose recognized the "let's change the subject" underlying his words. She stood up and smiled at him. "Only if you tell me all about the Atlanteans. Do they have gills?"

He burst out laughing, and a wave of warmth that felt far too much like contentment shimmered through her.

That's when her door slammed open, and the crazy man stormed into her kitchen.

8

ALEJANDRO'S GUN was in his hand almost before he realized he'd drawn it. The wild-eyed man who'd burst into Rose's house looked deranged. The red-rimmed eyes. The crazy bush of long gray hair. The bare feet.

The pink flamingos embroidered all over his bright green silk pajamas.

"Who the hell are you?" Alejandro demanded, moving to block the intruder's access to Rose.

"I am Harold, the one who will destroy you," the man said melodramatically, sneering and doing his best impression of a cartoon villain in one of the TV shows Mac's nephew liked to watch.

Alejandro, prepared for almost anything else, blinked. "Harold?"

Rose squeezed around Alejandro and stared at the guy. "Why?"

Harold paused, mid-sneer. "Why what?"

"Why are you going to destroy me?" Rose glanced at Alejandro, and she didn't look nearly worried enough to suit him.

Harold might be loco, but crazy people could still be very dangerous.

"Um. I don't actually know the answer to that," Harold said, biting his lip. "I'm under orders. I'm new."

Rose nodded like she understood, and Alejandro had to fight to keep from being impressed about how calm she was about the whole thing. Unless this kind of thing happened to her all the time? He'd never met a family of witches before, so who the hell knew?

"You need to leave. Now," Alejandro said, determined to take control of the situation. He was the P-Ops agent, after all. He tried not to think about how Mac would be laughing his ass off if he could see this. Mac's *stone* ass.

Alejandro gritted his teeth.

Rose gave Alejandro a *look*, and he knew that look. It was the universal female expression that meant "you're not helping." He narrowed his eyes at her, and she had the nerve to flash him a smile before turning back to the intruder.

"How about a cup of coffee, Harold?"

Alejandro groaned. "Do you routinely offer refreshment to crazy people who burst into your house and threaten you?"

"I don't do *anything* routinely," Rose said, and if it hadn't been for the threat of destruction, Alejandro almost would have thought she was flirting with him. Which was impossible, because what woman would flirt with a man who had a gun trained on a silk-pajama-clad intruder?

"You're almost as crazy as he is," he said, shaking his head, which was suddenly aching. If he spent much more time with Rose, he was going to need a bottle of pain relievers.

Or tequila.

"Hey, I'm not crazy," Harold interrupted. "I'm misunderstood."

Alejandro had to laugh. "Really? You can stand there in those clothes and say that with a straight face?"

"Coffee?" Rose held up a mug.

"Yes, please," Harold said politely. "Do you have artificial sweetener?"

"No, but I have raw sugar," Rose said to the crazy man who had just *threatened to destroy her.* "Please have a seat."

Harold sat down.

Alejandro swore under his breath and lowered his gun, beaten but not defeated. "Okay, if we're going to do this, who the hell are you and why did you burst in here like that? Harold what? Orders from who?"

Rose handed Harold his cup, and the man took a small sip before responding. "Wouldn't it be 'orders from whom'? I don't think 'orders from who' is grammatically correct."

"I. Will. Shoot. You," Alejandro said slowly, finally understanding the expression "I'm at the end of my rope" that Mac used so often.

"Veeno," Harold said hastily. "Harold Veeno. I'm not sure who issued the orders. We have an email loop."

"A what?"

Rose's façade of calm finally cracked a little. "An email loop. You have an *email loop,*" she said, her voice a little higher than normal. "What's it called? Assassins Are Us?"

"I'm not an assassin," Harold said, pouting his lips out a little. Alejandro might have thought the man's feelings were hurt, if he gave a shit whether or not the man's feelings were hurt.

Which he didn't.

And he still wanted to shoot him.

"Then what are you? And what was that 'destroy you' crap about?" Alejandro said, at the end of his patience. "And why the hell are you wearing that?"

Rose put a hand on Alejandro's arm, and he inhaled a long, deep breath.

"Start again. Make sense this time. Or I *will* shoot you," he told Harold.

The man turned a little pale and cleared his throat. "My name is Harold Veeno. I'm an actor. I have my SAM-G card."

Alejandro didn't know the acronym. "SAM-G?"

"Screen Actors with Magic Guild," Rose said.

Harold beamed. "Yes! It's the highest honor in my craft. Would you like to see it?" He started patting his pants, probably for the wallet that wasn't there, since he didn't have any pockets.

"Another time," Alejandro gritted out.

"Right. Well, we got a request from PETMA—but I don't know from whom at PETMA--that somebody put a scare in the Cardinal witches to make them stop hurting the basilisks," Harold blurted out all in a rush, darting a smirk at Alejandro during the "from whom" bit.

"I might shoot you just for fun," Alejandro said, aiming his widest smile at the man, who promptly fell off his chair.

"Now look what you did," Rose scolded, rushing over to the fallen psycho actor. "He fainted. You actually made him faint."

"What *I* did? This lunatic was threatening you for somebody he didn't even know for--" he paused. "What is PETMA?"

"People for the Ethical Treatment of Magical Animals," Rose told him as she checked Harold's pulse. "I can't believe you made a man pass out just from *smiling* at him."

Alejandro couldn't believe it, either. It usually took the careful application of fists or shotgun shells to put a man down. But Rose was acting like *he* was in the wrong, instead of the crazy man on her floor.

"You can't? How about *this* smile?" Alejandro put his gun back in its holster, circled her wrist with one hand, and pulled her up to stand in front of him. He smiled down at her and put every ounce of the combined frustration and attraction he was feeling into it. "Does this make you want to pass out?"

Heat flared in Rose's cheeks, and her beautiful blue eyes widened.

"It makes me want to kiss you," she admitted.

"I would never refuse a lady." He brushed his lips against hers, a gentle touch, meaning to do just that much and no more. But she tasted of sunlight and sweetness, and he went back in, deeper, harder, and took her mouth like his suddenly ragingly hard cock wanted to take her body.

Except they were in the kitchen. With a crazed lunatic, possibly assassin, out cold on the floor. The thought was more powerful than a cold shower, and he abruptly released her. He stepped back, trying to control his breathing, but then he realized that Rose was breathing hard, too.

"I must be the worst P-Ops agent in history," he said ruefully.

"It's probably a matter of practice," Harold offered from the floor, startling them both.

"I warned you," Alejandro said, and then he pulled out his gun and fired.

9

ROSE yelped, which was just as undignified as it sounded, and jumped away from Alejandro. "You shot Harold! Are you insane?"

Alejandro pointed at the still-open kitchen door. "No. I shot a warning shot over the head of the basilisk that was trying to sneak into the house. Harold's fine."

They both looked at Harold, who was unconscious again.

"He doesn't really have the stomach for this job, does he?" Rose murmured, almost fond of Harold at this point. So he was crazy, and he'd threatened her. So what? If he hadn't stormed into her kitchen, then maybe the Kiss That Rocked Rose's World never would have happened.

And *that* would be a tragedy.

Alejandro sighed. "What are we going to do?"

"I don't know," she said, suddenly feeling shy. "I think we need to at least explore this attraction, um, this . . . whatever this is between us."

"I meant about Harold. But definitely yes to the exploring." His smile faded as he looked at the door. "Once we fix Mac."

"Right. I'm calling my mom to deal with Harold, and then we'll start brewing more potion." Rose made the call, and for once her mother didn't ask seven million questions.

Several minutes later, Harold had recovered enough to sit up by the time Sue walked in.

"Why is your door hanging open, and what in the *world* is he wearing?" Rose's mother stopped dead in her tracks and stared at Harold, who smiled almost bashfully back at her.

"It was the closest thing to villain wear I had handy, since most of my costumes are at the dry cleaners," he explained, and Alejandro started smacking himself in the forehead, over and over.

"Flamingos?" Sue shook her head. "Not really scary. If you're into birds, I would have gone with hawks or something."

Rose rolled her eyes. "Hawks? Ravens would be far more frightening."

"This is the man who threatened your *daughter*, *Senora* Cardinal," Alejandro said in that low, dangerous tone. "He is lucky to be alive, let alone discussing his clothing choices."

In a heartbeat, Sue went from cheerful neighbor to terrifying and powerful witch, raising her hands in the air and beginning to chant in a low tone.

Rose knew the cadence of that chant. Harold was about to be very, very sorry. Possibly for the rest of his unexpectedly short life.

"Mom. It was mostly a misunderstanding. Harold is an actor. He'll tell you all about it. Take him away, so we can make more potion. Please." Rose put the plea in her voice as well as in her words, praying to the goddess that her mother would listen. She just didn't have the energy to rehash it all again.

Sue opened her mouth and then shut it. "Fine." She shot a shrewd glance at Alejandro and then smiled sweetly at Rose. "I'll just leave you two alone, shall I? Come on, Harold. Let's discuss how lucky you are to be alive over a cup of tea."

A befuddled and babbling Harold followed her mother out the door, keeping one fearful eye trained on Alejandro all the way.

"He was sure you would have shot him," Rose told Alejandro.

"He was right," Alejandro said. "I'm going to check on Mac again while you start that potion."

"He's going to be okay. I promise. I once heard of a person who stayed stone for nearly a year and came out of it just fine. He had a slight eye twitch and a pathological fear of pigeons afterward, but no other side effects," Rose said, trying to be reassuring.

From the expression on Alejandro's face when he stalked out the door, she'd failed badly at it.

By the time he came back in, she'd put together the potion ingredients, covered the pot, and set it aside to process.

"It will be ready by morning," she told him, tired but proud of her mastery of the difficult spell. "I really need something to eat. How about you?"

"I'll eat when Mac can," he said, scowling out the window. "This is my fault. I should have been more prepared, instead of falling for the initiation nonsense. I'm no untested rookie."

The meaning behind his gruff declaration struck Rose a little too hard, and her heart thumped in her chest. "You're used to taking care of everyone, aren't you?"

He didn't answer, just shifted restlessly, and she realized she wasn't the only one who was tired of being trapped in her kitchen.

"That's it. We're going for pizza," she announced. "There's nothing we can do until tomorrow, and I need food or I'll fall over."

"I don't want to go for pizza," he growled, suddenly menacing in the fading light of dusk. She hadn't yet turned on the lights, preferring to work her potion spells in natural light, and she hadn't realized how dark it was getting until now, when she had a real predator in her kitchen.

Hawks and ravens, nothing. Alejandro was a *dragon*.

Metaphorically speaking.

Wow. She really was reeling from that kiss. *Time to shake it off, Rose.*

So she shrugged, pretending a lightheartedness she was far from feeling. "See you later, then."

In one long stride, he was blocking her way. "You're not leaving without me. Basilisks in your yard and crazy actors breaking into your house. No. Forget it."

A delicious shiver ran through her at his protectiveness, but she hid her reaction to him behind a layer of cheerful defiance. "Come with me or move aside, Buster. Nobody keeps me from my pepperoni and extra cheese."

10

ALEJANDRO secured the back door, sent a silent mental apology to his partner, and then led the way through Rose's house to the front. He gestured for her to stay back while he cleared the yard and was surprised when she actually obeyed.

Obeyed. *Hah*. Not Rose. He already knew that she was a woman who would do something only if she decided it was what she wanted to do. Stubborn, proud, and confident. It was incredibly hot.

She was incredibly hot. And funny, smart, and loyal to her family.

He was in trouble.

"It's clear," he called out. She appeared, framed in the doorway for an instant, and a fierce rush of longing swept through him. If only he could have someone like her. A woman whose life was summer and sunshine; gardens and family. A woman whose most serious problem was an infestation of lizard-chickens, or a no-talent actor.

No, he corrected himself, driven to brutal honesty by her smile. Not *a* woman.

This woman.

"It's a short walk," she said, shaking him out of his ridiculous fantasies of a peaceful life. "Right around the corner. One of the best geographical features of the neighborhood."

"Pizza?"

"Pizza."

The little restaurant was bustling, and as soon as Alejandro smelled the tomato-and-cheese-scented air, he knew why.

Rose caught him sniffing the air. "It smells wonderful in here, doesn't it? Gianni and his family opened the restaurant more than a hundred years ago."

The restaurant looked like all of the other Italian restaurants that Mac and his other fellow rookies had dragged him to, all candlelight and red-and-white-checked tablecloths, but he'd never smelled anything like it. He wanted to grab a knife and fork and dive into the aromas as an appetizer, even before they got to the actual food. His stomach suddenly rumbled, and Rose laughed.

"Guess you're hungrier than you thought."

The host, a short, middle-aged man wearing a dark suit and a welcoming smile, patted Rose's cheek. "You bring Gianni a nice young man to inspect, my Rosa?"

Rose blushed, and Gianni turned his affable smile on Alejandro. "Welcome, welcome. Any friend of Rosa's and all that."

Alejandro nodded his thanks and started to follow Rose to the table, but Gianni's hand shot out and he grabbed Alejandro's arm in a punishing grip.

"I don't know you, but I know trouble. You've seen it, and you've dealt it," Gianni said in a low tone.

The man's eyes flashed gold, and Alejandro tensed to reach for his gun, but Gianni only shook his head. "You might want to watch yourself. You'd be dead before you hit the floor," the older man warned him. "I only want to tell you to have a nice dinner, and then get the hell away from Rosa. She's too good for you."

Alejandro laughed, but there was no amusement in it. "Don't you think I know that?"

After that admission, he'd had enough of being polite. He broke Gianni's hold with an ease that clearly surprised the man. "And *you* might want to watch yourself. Maybe I'd be dead, as you say, but I wouldn't be the only one."

Gianni nodded, and there was a hint of respect in it, but Alejandro wasn't fooling himself that he'd made a friend. And he already had far too many enemies, so he'd be happy to count this one a draw. "I'm glad she has you in her corner."

Alejandro made his way to their table, and he and Rose talked a little, about nothing much, until the food arrived. The pizza tasted even better than it smelled, and he devoured several slices before coming up for air. Rose, who'd eaten three slices herself, finally sighed and reluctantly put her napkin down.

"You were right. We needed food, and this was amazing," he said.

She nodded, but he could tell her mind was elsewhere. Far away from him, maybe. He was surprised by how much he didn't like that thought.

"Tell me about her," she said quietly. "The woman who left you for your friend."

Alejandro turned the question over in his mind as he studied her. The candlelight made her beautiful, but also different, in a less approachable way. *Too* beautiful. Too *not-for-him*.

He didn't like that, either, and he didn't understand why a woman he'd only met that morning was having such a strong impression on him.

"Maria," he finally said. "She was young and beautiful, and I think she wanted me because she was afraid, and I made her feel safe. Not because she loved me."

"I'm sorry. You must have loved her very much."

"Is that what your *gift* tells you?" He regretted his harsh tone the second he saw the hurt shimmer in her eyes, but he'd never known how to make pretty words or gentle speeches, and he was probably too old to learn the art now.

"I'm from a tiny town in Guatemala you've never heard of, and vampires killed most of my family and friends before I was old enough to learn how to fight back," he said flatly.

"That's horrible. I'm so sorry. I lost my father when I was young, too, not that I'm comparing a car accident to your village's overwhelming tragedy. I'm just saying that I know how hard it is to lose even one person you love."

"It is horrible. But it's in the past, and it's why I do what I do now." He shrugged, as if it didn't matter, but Rose probably saw right through his pathetic pretense.

Thankfully, she didn't call him on his crap.

"We've never had a problem with them here, because, well, witches. We're a pretty vibrant community, and the vamps in this region all know we can hurt them very badly if they ever try anything. So they leave us alone, and we leave them alone as long as they behave," Rose said.

"How *civilized* of you." The bitterness in his voice hung in the air between them.

"I'm sorry. It must sound horrible to you, but the vampires I know personally aren't like the ones who killed your family. They're just trying to figure out their place in a society that suddenly knows that they really exist," she said, and the kindness in her eyes disarmed him, making him want to be someone else. Someone who belonged in a place like this with Rose.

Someone he could never be.

She reached for his hand and held it in both of her own, and he knew he wasn't imagining the electric sense of connection between them, because her eyes flared wide at the sensation. In the soft candlelight, her eyes were dark pools of mystery. The curve of her cheek was a poem; the fall of her hair was a song.

But he had no talent for poem or song; he was nothing more than rage fashioned into a blunt weapon.

43

"I don't—I've never felt that before. And I don't understand why I do now. You're not even my type," she said, laughing a little but looking confused.

Anger flared through him at the thought of any other man being her *type*; a hot, almost feral emotion that he had no right to feel. "What is your type?"

"Nerdy guys with a good sense of humor, pretty much," she confessed. "And you're *so* not that."

He had to think for a few seconds to come up with the definition of nerdy, but then he smiled grimly. "No. Never that."

"She must have been crazy," Rose blurted out. "To leave you for anyone else. You're special. I've only known you a day, and I know that."

He didn't know what to do with the feelings she caused to rise up in him, so hopeful and tentative, so he pushed them aside, down deep where he kept painful memories and his knowledge of the viciously real nature of the world. But sunlight was the enemy of pain; it brightened shadowed corners and gave a gleaming polish to the battered edges of what he supposed might be called his soul.

So naturally he doubted it; his soul was long since blackened beyond repair. Ever since he'd shirked his duty to steal a private moment, and people had died because of it.

His fault.

His burden.

His guilt.

"We should get back," he said abruptly, standing up. "Your cat is still outside, yes? Who knows what the basilisks are doing to it."

Rose's small flinch of hurt added another scar to his burden, but he took it gladly. It was what he knew. What he was meant for. Not sunlight or hope, but vengeance.

"Bob is way too smart to get caught by the same trick twice, or I never would have let him roam," she said, raising her chin. "I'm sorry you think I'm so uncaring."

He reached out for her, but she turned away, and his hand missed her arm and touched the curve of her hip. A storm of want battered its way through him, and he had to fight not to let himself show it.

"I don't think that at all, Rose Cardinal. I think, instead, that you care too much," he said gently.

He put money on the table for the bill, and they walked back to her house in a silence that was far too vast to breach.

11

ROSE tossed and turned for a few restless hours, unable to sleep with Alejandro right down the hall. Her skin was still vibrating with the sensation of his touch on her hip; nerve endings she'd never felt before had flared into almost painful existence.

But her inability to sleep was caused by more than the physical wanting. He'd let her see him—really *see* him—and now she couldn't pretend, even to herself, that he was nothing more than an arrogant alpha male come to create havoc in her life.

Although the *havoc* part was true enough . . .

Impatient with herself, she threw off the blanket and took a quick shower, then dressed in her usual jeans and top and headed for the smell of freshly brewed coffee coming from her kitchen. Alejandro stood at the back door, staring out into the yard.

"They're getting bolder," he said without turning around, and she could read the anger in the straight, hard line of his stance without even seeing his face. "I had to chase a few of them off Mac. With all due respect to Astrid Buttercup, it was pretty hard not to shoot them."

"The potion should be ready by now. We can go turn Mac back into Mac, and you can be on your way to the next P-Ops problem." She wouldn't let the absence of this man disrupt her life. She *wouldn't*.

She couldn't.

Instead, she'd do something useful. She marched over to the cupboard and reached for the rack of clean vials, and then paused.

"No need to bottle this. Let's just take it all." She started to lift the heavy pot, but Alejandro was there first.

She followed him out to Mac's statue, which was almost pretty with touches of rose light on it, and wasn't even a little bit surprised to see her mother and grandmother heading toward them.

"We thought you could use the moral support, honey," Sue said, rushing up and giving Rose a hug. She aimed a narrow-eyed glance at Alejandro, who glared right back at her.

"Time to work some magic," Granny said, grinning madly. Her socks were back on her feet, instead of her elbows, at least.

Rose shook her head. Her family members might be maddening, but they were hers. Alejandro's story had given her the gift of appreciating them all a little bit more. She'd have that, still, after he was gone.

She squared her shoulders and took the lid of the pot. The sweet aroma of the sparkling pink potion wafted out into the early morning air, and she heard a loud meow from the side of the house.

"Bob's telling you that it smells good," Granny said.

Rose ignored her and focused on her mother's reaction.

Sue stared down at the potion and then closed her eyes and took a deep sniff. "Smells perfect, looks perfect—let's do this!"

Breathing a sigh of relief, Rose nodded to Alejandro. "Okay, you can pour it on him. Slowly and carefully, being sure to get as much on him as you can."

"One, two, three, *abracadabra*," Granny shouted.

Alejandro shot her a look. "I thought you said--"

"Witch humor," Rose said, sighing. "Just go ahead. And hope for the best."

It was triple the amount that should be needed. Just in case. But Rose surreptitiously crossed her fingers behind her back, anyway, as Alejandro carefully poured the entire pot of potion on his partner's stone head.

They all took a step back when the statue started to shake and shudder.

"Thank goodness," Sue said, beaming. "I knew--"

"Too soon, Mom," Rose snapped. "Look."

And Rose's heart sank to somewhere in the vicinity of her ankles, because the statue was settling back down, and the tremors were subsiding.

And Mac was still stone.

Alejandro abruptly turned and hurled her potion pot across the garden. It smashed into a low stone wall with a resounding crash, but the noise was almost drowned out by the sound of Alejandro loudly and viciously cursing in at least two different languages.

"I'm so sorry," Rose said. "I don't know—we'll brew another potion. I'll get Mom and Granny to help, we'll--"

"What were you doing when you were supposed to be brewing this so carefully last night?" Sue put her hands on her hips and stared down her nose at her daughter; a neat trick since she was several inches shorter than Rose.

Rose, who'd been on the last frayed edge of calm all night, threw her hands up in the air. "Sex, Mom. We were having hot, sweaty, fabulous sex all night. There. Are you happy?"

She stalked over to Alejandro, grabbed his face in her hands and planted a hot, R-rated, definitely-don't-do-in-front-of-your-mother kiss on him and then fled to the house before she burst into tears. The last thing she heard before she reached the refuge of her kitchen was Granny's long whistle and Alejandro's terse announcement.

"Now, I think we call the Atlanteans."

12

ALEJANDRO called a number that Lord Justice had once given him—a number that he'd never used. The line rang twice, and then a sequence of clicks and beeps sounded, and then the line went dead, and he was left listening to dial tone.

Well. He'd known better than to expect help from anyone but himself. Now he just had to figure out how the hell to work magic and save his partner.

"Incoming," Granny sang out, and she and Sue both took several steps away from the statue.

Alejandro looked around, ready to draw his gun, but he didn't see anything. "What are you talking about?"

Sue pointed to the area just to the left of Mac, where an oval shimmer of light was starting to form.

"I thought you warded this garden against magical entry," Rose's grandmother accused.

Sue nodded, rolling up her sleeves. "I did. Watch out."

Alejandro looked at the oval again and grinned. He held up a hand before Sue could try to blast it.

"It's okay. It's the cavalry."

Lord Justice of Atlantis, half-brother to the king, stepped through first. His long braid of swirling blue and black hair still reached his waist, and his very deadly sword still stuck up from its scabbard on his back. His sharp gaze swept the area before returning to Alejandro, and he bowed.

"You called us, and we came," he said, and Alejandro knew it was just as likely that the "us" referred to the dual natures of Justice's personality as it did to actual other people. But Ven stepped through the portal, and then Alaric, and Alejandro blew out a sigh of relief.

Now things would definitely work out. The King's Vengeance, also King Conlan's brother, and Alaric, High Priest of Atlantis, were each as deadly and magically powerful on their own as Lord Justice. The trio? Unstoppable.

"Thank you," Alejandro said when the portal winked out of existence, so he knew nobody else was coming through. "I have a big problem."

"Oh, honey, you are a cutie patootie," Granny told Alaric, sidling up to him.

Alejandro's head nearly exploded at the sight of the expression on the face of the five-hundred-year-old high priest—the most powerful Atlantean of all time, or so he'd heard—as Rose's grandmother leered at him.

Alaric's green gaze was ice. Grown men would run screaming for their mothers at the sight of that gaze. "I beg your pardon, Sorceress?"

Granny grinned and reached up and pinched Alaric's cheek.

Ven howled with laughter. Howled. There was no other word for it. He doubled over and slapped his knee and still kept laughing.

"We prefer witch, Wizard," Sue said, still unhappy with the intrusion into her territory, Alejandro guessed from the look on her face.

He hastened to make introductions. "*Senora* Cardinal, *Abuelita* Cardinal, please allow me to present Lord Alaric, High Priest of Atlantis, and Lord Ven and Lord Justice, brothers to the king."

Sue nodded. "Pleased to meet you," Sue said, sounding anything but.

"Welcome to the home of the Cardinal witches, boys," Granny said, chuckling. "We don't get royalty around here much, if you don't count the new Burger Emperor place downtown. I hope you don't expect me to curtsy. Bad knees since the 1980s."

Alejandro suppressed the urge to clutch his head, but Ven just started laughing again.

"Oh, I love you, ma'am," Ven told Granny. "Please, call me Ven. I think we're going to be great friends."

"I don't need friends. I find them burdensome," Alaric said, nodding briefly to the two witches and then walking over to the statue. "Basilisk? You tried the usual potions?"

Sue stepped up next to him, professional interest apparently winning out over annoyance, and the two of them started talking remedies.

Justice drew his sword. "We will do a perimeter sweep," he announced, before striding off.

"Still warm and fuzzy as ever, as you see," Ven told Alejandro, who had to smile.

"I don't understand 'fuzzy,' but I think I get your meaning."

"So, we're glad to help, but aren't they a little old for you?" Ven jerked his head a little toward the witches. "We need to find you a woman your own age."

Alejandro's spine tingled with the awareness of being watched, and he slowly turned around to see Rose staring at him. The imprint of that wild, sexy kiss she'd given him burned on his lips and every fiber of his being screamed *want*. *Need*.

Mine.

"Oh, hello, Gorgeous. I begin to understand a lot more," Ven said, bowing deeply toward Rose.

Possessiveness like nothing he'd ever known roared through Alejandro. "Stay away from her, *Your Majesty*, or I will kick your royal ass for you," he growled.

Ven turned amused eyes to him. "So, it's like that, is it? You're toast, buddy. Be sure to invite us to the wedding."

Rose, who hopefully hadn't heard any of that, clenched her hands into fists at her sides and marched into the garden right toward them. "Who are you, and what the hell is going on?"

Her voice cut through everything else, and Alaric swung around to stare at her. "I the hell am the one who is going to fix your problem. I only have personal acquaintance with one witch, but you are apparently her equal in your ability to annoy me. I advise you to be quiet and learn something."

Rose turned pink and then white, and her entire body started to vibrate. Alejandro took a careful step back before she exploded.

Ven just grinned. "I apologize for Alaric. He woke up on the wrong side of the century, and he's grumpy whenever he travels without his wife, poor baby."

Alaric simply sighed, clearly well used to Ven's jibes.

Alejandro repeated his introductions, and Rose's eyes widened as she stared back and forth between Ven and Alaric. "Really? Atlanteans in my garden? This is definitely a weekend for the record books."

Alaric beckoned Rose over, and Alejandro took her hand in his, earning him a surprised and grateful look that he tucked away to be remembered later, when he was alone again.

"You are not at fault, Sorceress," Alaric said.

"I'm not a sorceress," Rose said.

"You're *my* sorceress," Alejandro murmured, feeling like an idiot when she shot him a shocked look. He hadn't expected her to hear that.

Hadn't actually expected to *say* it.

Damn.

"We're witches, honey buns," Granny said, and Alaric scowled, earning him a fresh wave of laughter from Ven.

"Yeah, they're witches, *honey buns*," Ven said.

Alaric casually flipped a hand into the air, formed an energy sphere, and then hurled it at Ven. It smacked the prince in the arm, hard.

"Ouch," Ven drawled.

"What do you mean, it's not my fault?" Rose interjected. "The potion didn't work. Of course it's my fault."

Alaric shook his head. "No. It is not, although you are clearly well-mated to Alejandro, since both of you insist on claiming blame for guilt that is not yours."

Rose gasped. "I'm not mated to anybody--"

"We didn't do anything," Alejandro said, at the same time, as he watched Sue's frown reappear.

Granny just chuckled. "It's about time. That girl has needed a good man for a while. You know the saying: a hard man is good to find."

"Granny!" Rose covered her face with one hand for a moment, and then sighed. "Alaric. Your Priestlyness. Please continue."

"And we need to get rid of the basilisk infestation," Alejandro added.

Justice rounded the corner of the house just then, and Rose's mouth fell open.

"He's married. And possibly schizophrenic," Alejandro growled.

Rose tried to yank her hand away, but he tightened his fingers on hers. She gave him a look, but quit struggling.

"Are you insane?" she finally asked, her tone sweetly and falsely polite. "Did the P-Ops training rot your brain?"

"No, but you might," he muttered, shaking his head to clear it of thoughts of her lush body wrapped around anybody but him. That kiss had clearly destroyed his ability to reason.

She edged as far away as she could get while he still had her hand.

"Rose Cardinal, Lord Justice. Lord Justice, Rose Cardinal," he said, realizing he sounded rude and not giving much of a damn.

Justice bowed and Alejandro scowled at him. Justice and Ven exchanged a glance, and then Justice grinned. "We see. You have found your Keely."

Granny looked interested. "What is a Keely? And how did you get your hair that gorgeous color?"

"Keely is our wife, and our hair is the result of our half-Nereid nature," Justice told her. "We will take care of the basilisks with our sword now, since we must return to Keely."

"That's not the royal we, that's the two sides of his charming personality talking," Ven offered, when all three Cardinal witches stared at Justice.

"You can't kill the basilisks," Rose said.

"Oh, no," Sue agreed. "You kill those creatures over my daughter Buttercup's dead body."

"Where should we put it?" Alaric asked.

Alejandro stared at him. "Put what?"

"The child's dead body," Alaric said, but then he seemed to catch on pretty quickly that he'd gotten it wrong when Sue threatened to 'cut his priestly balls off with her kitchen shears'."

"STOP," Rose shouted. "There will be no killing and no castration. But for the love of the goddess, will somebody please tell me how to fix Alejandro's partner?"

"Your bay laurel was from a stunted tree," Alaric said, which meant nothing to Alejandro but obviously meant something to Rose and her family.

"You have magic powerful enough to tell that by just looking at the residue on the statue?" Granny hugged herself and chuckled. "Hoo boy, if you weren't already married, I'd make a run for you myself."

"I don't *have* magic. I *am* magic," Alaric announced.

Ven rolled his eyes. "The same way he *is* arrogant."

Alaric lifted a hand in warning, and Ven grinned.

"Okay, okay. You don't have to blast me again," the prince said, surrendering. "Just fix the stone man so we can get going. Erin and I are going out to lunch."

"Lord Vengeance's wife is also a witch," Justice told Rose.

She nodded politely, although Alejandro could see that she was itching to get on with transforming Mac. "And what is your wife?"

"She is an archaeologist," Justice proudly proclaimed.

"I never thought I'd get to meet an Atlantean," Sue said wonderingly, her hostility apparently gone.

"And Mac?" Alejandro asked, getting a little edgy himself, although he had confidence in the Atlanteans after what he, Justice, and Keely had been through in Las Pinturas.

"Yes. Mac." Alaric called a dancing wave of shimmering blue water through the air to himself and then twirled one finger and sent it swooping and dancing around the statue of Alejandro's partner.

Rose watched, fascinated. "Is the precise movement of the water important to your magic?"

Alaric finally allowed himself to smile. "Not at all. It just looks impressive. And here is your human."

The water vanished and Mac, fully himself again, stood staring at everyone gathered around him.

Alejandro let Rose's hand go and hurried over to grab his partner's arm. "Mac! Are you all right?"

Mac blinked. "Mommy?"
Alejandro caught him when he collapsed.

13

"HE WILL NEED TO SLEEP for at least a day, maybe two. I will send him to Sue Cardinal's couch," Alaric said. He gestured, and Mac vanished.

"Thank you so much," Rose said, impulsively hugging the high priest who was also a miracle worker.

Alejandro made a low growling noise in the back of his throat, and Ven, the funny one, started to laugh again.

"You are amazing," Sue said.

Alaric nodded. "Yes."

Granny grinned again. "And humble."

"Mom, let's go take care of the agent," Sue said. "You can flirt with Atlantean high priests another time.

Alaric watched them hurry off, and then he shook his head. "I can only hope not," he said, shuddering just a little.

Rose smiled at the high priest. "Granny is fairly formidable."

"Yes," Alaric said again, this time more fervently.

Justice called the portal, and the familiar oval shape started to shimmer into existence. "Until next time, our friend," he said, nodding to Alejandro.

"Thank you. I am in your debt," Alejandro said.

"The debt is ours, and can never be repaid," Justice replied. "Until next time."

With that, he stepped into the portal and vanished. Ven paused for a moment and glanced out at the garden and then back at Rose.

"My wife might be able to help you with your basilisk problem—in a humane way," he offered, and Rose sighed with relief.

"That would be amazing. Thank you."

"I'll be in touch, Alejandro. Keep your woman close to you; she's a keeper," he said, and then he grabbed Rose's hand and kissed it. "You take care of our boy, Rose Cardinal."

Rose, blushing, stammered out an incoherent response and then managed to form an actual sentence. "I'm not his woman."

Ven threw back his head and laughed. "That's what all of our wives used to say."

With that little nugget of wisdom, he vanished through the portal, too.

Alaric was the last to go, and he stopped and took Rose's chin in his hand. "Interesting. Your magic resonates with that of Alejandro. No wonder you are so well mated."

"We're not mated," she protested, but then the first part of his comment pierced the fog in her sleep-deprived brain. "His magic? He has magic?"

Alejandro looked stunned. "I don't have magic."

"Of course you do," Alaric told him. "Have you ever missed a shot, even once?"

Alejandro paused and thought about it for a minute. "Not when I've been really aiming," he said slowly, a look of disbelief dawning on his face. "Not even once, since I was eight years old."

Alaric nodded. "There is magic in the world even older than Atlantis. The magic that infuses a guardian who has survived trial by fire and blood. This is what burns inside you, Alejandro."

Alejandro sighed, his shoulders slumping, and Rose wanted nothing more than to hold him, right at that moment. Maybe forever.

"I'm tired of the darkness, my friend," Alejandro said. "I find myself wishing for sunshine and peace."

"I think you have found her, as I found my own Quinn, although I wonder what she would say if she heard me refer to her as sunshine," Alaric said, a smile slowly curving his lips.

Rose had to admit the high priest was totally gorgeous, in a "scary, hot guy you meet in your nightmares" kind of way, when he wasn't being an arrogant ass. All three of the Atlanteans had been hunky males of the supreme alpha variety, just like Alejandro.

She glanced at her P-Ops agent and amended the thought. Well, not nearly as beautiful as Alejandro.

"Thank you again--"

"He's gone," Alejandro said. "He doesn't like long goodbyes. Or, actually, any goodbyes."

Rose nodded. "I--"

He yanked her to him and swallowed whatever she'd been about to say with his mouth, taking hers in a long, hard, almost brutal kiss. She was helplessly clutching his shoulders by the time he raised his head.

"If you ever look at another man that way, I might have to shoot him," he warned, his dark eyes heating up. "And as you just heard, I never miss."

Rose was, for maybe the first time in forever, speechless. "You—I—you—You are a complete *ass*," she finally sputtered.

He shrugged, and in that moment he was every inch the arrogant male predator that she'd avoided all her life. She didn't understand why it seared a bolt of red-hot desire straight through her, but it did. Oh, yeah. It certainly did.

He leaned in close, and she had to clamp her lips shut to keep from kissing him again.

"Maybe," he said. "But I'm tired of fighting it. I've never felt like this about anybody in my entire life. So, yeah, I'm a complete ass. But I'm *your* complete ass. Deal with it."

She did the rational, adult thing. She was Rational Rose, right?

She bolted.

14

WHEN she turned and ran, Alejandro thought about surrendering. Hadn't the world gone to hell enough in the past eleven years, now that vampires, shape-shifters, and witches were all real? Maybe Rose Cardinal was too much for him, and he should simply raise the white flag, lie down, and surrender.

Except, he wasn't the surrendering kind.

He took a moment to enjoy the fierce rush of anticipation, and then he exploded out of his casual stance into a flat-out run, never slowing for a second as he caught up to Rose just around the side of the house, lifted her up, and threw her over his shoulder. Then he kept running, ignoring her shouts and the feel of her fists pounding on his back.

"Now," he said grimly. "We are going to have a little talk."

Rose couldn't believe it. The overbearing, arrogant, possessive, absolutely too . . . too . . . *male* man had thrown her over his *shoulder.* As if he were a primitive warrior claiming his captured princess.

Well, this princess was a witch, and it was about time he learned that in a much more up-close-and-personal manner. She narrowed her eyes as he turned left, into the entrance of the park near her house, and she cast a little spell. The tiniest of spells, really.

She made his pants disappear.

He stumbled to a halt, swearing a blistering streak of words in a string of English, Spanish, and maybe even something else, and dumped her none-too-gently on her butt on the grass. This meant that her view, front and center, was of the bountiful goodness that the goddess had graced him with, and she hadn't even planned it that way.

And from this angle, she could tell that at least part of him was definitely happy to see her. Luckily, the park was officially closed until ten, and her neighbors were rule followers, so the slight worry that a child would get the shock of a lifetime was fleeting.

Her breath caught in her throat, and she tried to ignore the thudding of her heart. Yes, he was incredibly hot, damn him. All broad shoulders, amazing rippling muscles, and dark, dangerous eyes. She tried to be mature and keep her eyes off the hard curves of his massive thigh muscles--and what stood so proudly between them--but she was having a very hard time of it.

Hard time. Oh, boy. Now her brain had melted into bad pun land.

Alejandro still wore his boots, shirt, and even his gun--in a complicated back holster --but the pants were definitely gone; oh, yes, they were.

She forced her gaze up past his impressive endowment to meet his eyes, and she licked her lips. His eyes darkened with something primal; a powerful emotion that touched the purely feminine part of her soul . When he crouched down next to her, looming over her like the predator he was, she made very certain to lean toward him, instead of away.

Never, ever let them see you're intimidated--it was the law with jungle cats, right?

"Is that what you want? Right here and now?" he challenged her. "Then strip down, because I've thought of nothing else but being inside you for every second of every minute since I met you."

Her breath hitched, and her body tightened and loosened all at once; nerve endings zinging with the electricity that had crackled between them since they'd met, even before she'd been willing to acknowledge it.

"The whole day and a half since we met?" She bit her lip, hard, against the urge to reach out and stroke him. All of him.

"Some things you just know," he said implacably, and her heart cried out *yes, yes, yes!*

But her stubborn mind was still sticking with *no*.

Stupid mind.

She concentrated hard and made his pants reappear on his body. Then she stood up, brushed off the grass, and shook her head. "How can I trust something that happened so fast? It's impossible."

She walked away, leaving him standing there alone, and it was the hardest thing she'd ever done.

15

ALEJANDRO watched the woman he'd fallen in love with walk away from him, and his world collapsed around him. She was right. It was impossible.

But it was true—a truth stronger than any he'd ever known. Maybe it was fate, maybe it was magic. He didn't care how she labeled it.

He just knew she was his.

He went after her again, but this time he let her reach her house before he caught up to her.

"What do you want?" she asked despairingly.

"I want everything," he growled.

He wanted to kiss her. He wanted to shake her. He wanted to fall to his knees and beg.

He started with the kiss. He backed her up against the wall, step by slow step, giving her every chance to tell him no. It would kill him if she did, but no was no.

Always.

She didn't say it. He offered a silent prayer of thanks, because she *didn't say no.*

He put his hands on either side of her head, caging her in, and she still didn't say no. She was beautiful and defiant and strong, and she was his.

He just had to make *her* see it.

He stared down into her beautiful, mysterious, dangerous eyes.

"Trust this," he growled, and then he took her mouth with every ounce of passion and heat inside him.

She gasped a little, and he tasted her breath, swallowing the sound. He pulled her closer to his body, which craved her like a parched man craves crystal clear water. A roaring wave of possessiveness demanded he hold her--keep her--never let her walk away from him again.

Her hands tensed on his arms and then, gloriously, wondrously, she put them around his neck and arched her soft curves into him in a clear signal of acceptance. Surrender.

Maybe even a matching hunger.

He drove his tongue into her mouth, claiming her. A kind of insanity raged through him. She'd dared to walk away from him, taking the sunlight with her.

He had to make sure that she never would again.

Madness seized him, and he lifted her up and sat her on the coffee table, not knowing what he was doing, only knowing in some primal, predatory side of his own nature that he wanted to be even closer. He pushed her knees apart and stepped between them, sliding his hands down the soft denim of her worn jeans from knee to hip, still kissing her. His erection was so hard it hurt, and he put his hands on her ass to pull her toward him; to put his cock, though still in his pants, exactly where he needed it to be.

The clothes between them were maddening, and he knew she'd be warm and wet underneath them, but he couldn't bear to release her long enough to remove them. Madness still gripped him in its clawed and fanged grip, and he was desperate to hold her, touch her, drive inside her until they both collapsed.

Part of him knew that it was wrong—too soon, not rational, it didn't make any sense at all--he knew it, but he didn't care. All he knew was how much he needed her, and it was all he could do to keep from ripping her shirt down the front in order to expose the silken skin of her breasts to his gaze. She murmured or moaned, a tiny sound, and tightened her hold on him, and he was lost.

"I need you," he said roughly, his voice like sandpaper. "I don't know why or how, but I do. Please. *Please.*"

She put her hands on his face and pulled back a little to study his face, and the wildness and desire he saw in her unbelievably blue eyes drove him over the brink of the abyss.

"Yes," she said. One tiny word that changed his entire world.

Rose reveled in her boldness. She was acting nothing like herself. Or maybe she was acting *exactly* like herself. Either way, she wanted this man and this moment. She didn't know how to believe his claims of love and forever, but she wanted to believe.

Oh, how she wanted to believe.

"Bedroom," she gasped, just before he ripped her shirt down the middle and then fastened his lips on her nipple, right through her bra, right there in the middle of her living room. Anybody could walk in, this was crazy, this was . . .

He sucked, hard. She screamed and forgot about anything else beyond the feel of his mouth on her.

He lifted her up, still licking and sucking her nipple, and she instinctively wrapped her legs around his waist and hung on as he strode down the hall to her bedroom.

"Yes, please, more," she said, gasping or whimpering or crying out, only the goddess knew which, and he tossed her on the bed and then stripped out of his clothes.

"You're so beautiful," she whispered, and he laughed.

"No, my sorceress, my witch, my lovely one. You are the beautiful one." He pulled off her shoes and then her jeans, fumbling in his haste, and it was her turn to laugh.

"We have time," she said, but then she frowned. "Mac?"

"Alaric said he'll sleep for a day or two. Alaric is never wrong," Alejandro said, and then he pounced on her.

His body was all hard muscle and elegant lines, and she was finally free to touch. So she did. His hot skin was a paler shade of copper where his pants had covered him, and the dark trail of hair that led down the rippling muscles of his abdomen pointed an arrow at the impressively large and deliciously hard part of him that had so intrigued her in the park.

"I don't have much practice at this," she said, suddenly afraid she'd disappoint him, and his face lit up with a huge smile.

"Neither do I. Let's figure it out together."

Alejandro was almost afraid she'd disappear right in front of his eyes. She was too wonderful to be real; too warm, too beautiful, too kind, too *everything*. He wanted to taste and touch every inch of her skin—brand her with his touch until she screamed his name and begged him to stay.

"I want you now," he said, and he didn't even recognize his own voice. "I need you. Now."

"Yes," she said again, and he touched and tasted and licked and sucked until she came, hard, in his hands and in his mouth, again and again, and then when he couldn't stand it any longer, not for one single second more, he plunged into her hot, wet heat and finally, *finally*, he was where he belonged.

Rose wrapped her arms and legs around him and murmured encouragement, but the heat shimmering in her eyes was all the goad he needed.

"Please. Now," she said, and he thrust home, again and again, harder and harder, until his cock was harder than it had ever been in his life and he was a heartbeat away from going over the edge. But he wanted to take her with him. He slowed to an exquisitely careful pace and reached down between them to touch that sensitive bud of nerves that he'd already learned so well.

"Come for me, *querida*," he whispered, and she exploded around him; her feminine muscles clenching around his cock as her orgasm took her flying over the edge into ecstasy. Then he shouted her name over and over as he came harder than he'd even known was possible, pumping more and more of his seed into her body, until he thought he might die of pleasure.

They lay on their sides, facing each other, for minutes or hours or maybe years, until both of them could breathe again.

"Now you have to marry me," he told her seriously. "You might be pregnant with baby Alejandro right at this very minute."

She started to laugh, which caused her breasts to jiggle so interestingly that his cock took notice and began to get hard again.

"I'm a witch, Alejandro. We don't get pregnant unless we want to," she said, her eyes dancing.

"Fair enough. Then marry me because you love me."

16

ROSE almost fell off the bed. "I what? You could teach Alaric lessons in arrogance. Just because we had the hottest sex I've ever had in my life--"

"Or ever will, at least until the next time, which might be soon if you keep causing your lovely breasts to bounce like that," he said, matching action to words and bending down to suck her nipple into his mouth.

She gasped and her head fell back. The man was a sex god. There was just no other way to put it. "You—you have to stop that. Oh, wow. Okay, maybe not just yet."

He slid his clever fingers between her legs, and she surrendered completely. "Never mind. Don't stop. Don't—oh, goddess—don't stop."

He didn't.

By the next time they were able to catch their breath, it was almost six o'clock in the evening, and Rose freaked out when she caught sight of the clock.

"My mother—Mac—oh, no," she moaned. "They'll think I've turned into a crazed sex fiend."

"Have you?" Alejandro asked, extremely interested in the answer. "Because I think I could go one more round, if we--"

"No!" She jumped out of bed. "We have to, I need to, if we--"

"I love you," he said simply, interrupting her wild babbling, and she froze.

"You what?"

"I love you. I've never met anyone like you, and I never will." He stood up and crossed the room until he stood only a few inches away from her. "You're brave and smart, and funny and loyal. You love your crazy grandmother and your lunatic sister, and you even care about the fate of lizard-chickens."

The look on her face was one of pure astonishment, but he didn't see any hint of rejection, so he took a deep breath, gathered what was left of his courage, and pushed ahead.

"I don't know if it's because of our magic, like Alaric said--"

"He's never wrong," she said wryly.

"Or because some part of your soul is perfectly matched to mine, but I love you and I need you. Marry me, my witch, my enchantress, my sorceress. Be mine. I will be faithful to you forever, and I will love you for all eternity."

The absolute *rightness* of every word he was saying rang out, loud and clear, and Alejandro had never been so certain of anything in his life.

He knelt down, still stark naked, and smiled up at the woman who'd stolen his heart. "Marry me."

Rose's eyes widened, and an expression of pure wonder crossed her face. "I finally know," she said, almost reverently. "Your deepest desire. It's *me*."

Relief flooded through him. "Of course."

"But how . . ."

"Maybe all we needed was love."

Rose opened her mouth and then shut it again, and then she blinked and looked around the room and back down at him.

"You can't propose to me when we're naked," she said firmly. "Go take a shower and get dressed, and then we will go out to the garden and do this again."

Her meaning took a minute to penetrate his brain, and then he leapt up and pulled her into his arms. "You love me," he said triumphantly, and she smiled a secret, deliciously feminine smile.

"Maybe. Now, shower."

"Only if you come with me."

It turned out that she would. So it was actually another hour later when Alejandro Vasquez, fully dressed, stood in the middle of her beautiful garden and asked Rose Cardinal to marry him.

This time she said yes.

EPILOGUE

Atlantis, six months later

ROSE AND HER HUSBAND sat on a low stone wall and watched, from a safe distance, as a flock of basilisks ran and played in the fantastically beautiful palace garden.

"This was the perfect solution," she said, leaning against him, still a little drunk on the high of their most recent round of lovemaking, which had taken place in their very own guest suite in the Atlantean palace. She almost had to pinch herself to believe that it was true, but then Queen Riley walked by carrying her son and waved.

To Rose.

"A queen of a mythical lost continent just waved to me," she said wonderingly. "To me, little Rose Cardinal of the Cardinal witches from Ohio."

Alejandro grinned. "Not so mythical or lost anymore. Maybe you should wave back."

"Oh! Right!" She did, enthusiastically, and then her gaze returned to the basilisks, and the shimmer of the magical force field around their enclosure. "They're perfectly safe here, and they can't hurt anyone."

Alejandro shook his head. "Who would have believed that the head gardener of this wonderland could actually be almost legally blind?"

"He sees with his magic, not his eyes," Rose told him, although he already knew, of course. "Basilisks will never be able to affect him, and he told me he actually likes them a lot. Treats them as pets."

Alejandro pulled her closer and kissed her again, and her heartbeat sped up like it did every single time he kissed her.

"Speaking of pets, I think we should get a dog to play with Bob," Alejandro said. "I've always wanted a dog. And you owe me, since Gianni glares at me every time we go for pizza."

It was true. Gianni had never gotten over his initial dislike of Alejandro. Maybe someday. The man *was* more than a hundred years old. It might just take some time.

"Dog?" Alejandro prompted.

"We can," Rose said slowly. "But we might be a little busy in a few months, so maybe we can adopt an older dog who won't be as demanding."

Alejandro, enjoying his first vacation from his new job at the Cincinnati office of P-Ops, looked puzzled. "What do you mean? Big witches conclave? Granny secretly planning to learn how to drive race cars?"

Rose smiled and shared another, altogether different secret, and then she had to kiss away the single tear that her big, strong, alpha male husband let fall as he placed his hand on her belly and the new life starting inside her.

"Together, forever," he said, his voice husky, repeating the words he told her every single day. The words that were inscribed inside her wedding ring.

"Maybe our baby can be friends with the little prince," she said, and then she froze. "Do you remember--"

"Your grandmother's prophecy?"

"Oh, no. 'Your eldest child will rule in an isle of myth'," Rose said. "You don't think—surely not?"

"This we worry about much, *much* later," Alejandro said firmly.

She laughed and kissed him with all the love in her heart, and then she shared another secret. "So, you know how I've been talking about going into business with a line of potions for every conversational need? I found a possible business partner, and I set up a meeting for when we get home. I'd love for you to meet him, but you have to promise not to shoot him."

Alejandro tilted his head. "Why in the world would I even think about shooting your new business partner?"

Rose grinned at him. "Mac told me you might try to shoot him. Because, and keep an open mind here--"

"Just *tell* me," her wonderful, sexy, impatient husband urged.

"He's actually kind of a troll."

THANK YOU

Thank you!

Thanks so much for reading *Alejandro's Sorceress*. I hope you had as much fun reading it as I did writing it.

Newsletter! Would you like to know when my next book is available? You can sign up for my new release e-mail list at www.alyssaday.com, follow me on twitter at @alyssa_day, or Like my Facebook page at facebook.com/authoralyssaday

Review it. My family hides the chocolate if I don't mention that reviews help other readers find new books, so if you have the time, please consider leaving one for *Alejandro's Sorceress*. I appreciate all reviews, whether positive or negative.

Try my other books! You can find excerpts of all of my books at www.alyssaday.com.

ABOUT THE AUTHOR

Alyssa Day is the pen name (and dark and tortured alter ego) of RITA award-winning and RWA honor roll member author Alesia Holliday. As Alyssa, she writes the *New York Times* best-selling **Warriors of Poseidon** paranormal series & **League of the Black Swan** paranormal romance/urban fantasy series and the upcoming **Cardinal Witches** series, and is the winner of the RT BookClub Reviewers Choice Award for Best Paranormal Romance of 2012.

As Alesia Holliday, she writes comedies that make readers snort things out of their noses, and is the author of the award-winning memoir about military families during war-time deployments: EMAIL TO THE FRONT.

As Lucy Connors, she writes gritty contemporary romance novels for teens (www.lucyconnors.com).

She's a diehard Buckeye who graduated *summa cum laude* from Capital University Law School and practiced as a trial lawyer in multi-million dollar litigation for several years before coming to her senses and letting the voices in her head loose on paper. She lives somewhere near an ocean with her Navy Guy husband, two kids, and any number of rescue dogs. Please visit Alyssa at www.alyssaday.com, follow her on Twitter (she's very chatty there!), or friend her on Facebook (warning: dog photos regularly appear).

BOOKS BY ALYSSA DAY

THE WARRIORS OF POSEIDON SERIES:

Atlantis Rising
Wild Hearts in Atlantis (a novella; originally in the WILD THING anthology)
Atlantis Awakening
Shifter's Lady (a novella; originally in the SHIFTER anthology)
Atlantis Unleashed
Atlantis Unmasked
Atlantis Redeemed
Atlantis Betrayed
Vampire in Atlantis
Heart of Atlantis
Alejandro's Sorceress (a related novella)

THE LEAGUE OF THE BLACK SWAN SERIES:

The Cursed
The Curse of the Black Swan (a novella; originally in the ENTHRALLED anthology)
The Unforgiven (coming soon)
The Unforgotten (coming in 2015)

THE CARDINAL WITCHES SERIES:

Alejandro's Sorceress (a novella)
Denal's Enchantress (coming in 2015)

SHORT STORY COLLECTION   *   NONFICTION

Random   Email to the Front

Made in the USA
Lexington, KY
13 January 2016